The Best Korean Short Stories – 1

THE CRUEL CITY
and Other Korean Short Stories

THE CRUEL CITY
and Other Korean Short Stories

The Si-sa-yong-o-sa Publishers, Inc., Korea
Pace International Research, Inc., U.S.A.

Published simultaneously in KOREA and the UNITED STATES

KOREA EDITION
First printing 1983
The Si-sa-yong-o-sa Publishers, Inc.
5-3 Kwanchol-dong, Chongno-ku
Seoul 110, Korea

U.S. EDITION
First printing 1983
Pace International Research, Inc.
Tide Avenue, Falcon Cove
P.O. Box 51, Arch Cape
Oregon 97102, U.S.A.

ISBN: 0-89209-212-2

This series is a co-publication by The Si-sa-yong-o-sa Publishers, Inc.
and The International Communication Foundation.

We hope that this collection of short stories may stimulate foreign readers to take interest in Korean literature and Korean culture. We also hope that it may introduce them to other literary works by Korean writers.

Translator's Preface

The publishing of even this small collection of my translations has felt somewhat like giving birth to a child, a process with which I have also had experience. The sense of relief and accomplishment, however, compensate for the discomfort of the gestation and birth.

My first attempt at translation, O Yong-su's "Yun-i and the Ox," was mainly for the purpose of language study. Now, after having translated more than a dozen short stories and a novel I am, of course, no longer satisfied with that first translation. Each time that I reread it I want to change phrases and words. It is much the same with these stories. I keep wanting to redo them in order to better express what I think the author is trying to convey, or to improve my writing. There comes a time, however, when the process of translation must cease.

Translation is a laborious task, but somewhere along the way the excitement of unraveling the literature of another language and people takes over and one is captured by the sheer fascination of the exercise.

I have two reasons for allowing my translation "child" to leave home now and appear before the eyes of those who will read this collection. I hope to introduce Korean literature to a wider reading audience and also to help that audience gain an understanding and an appreciation of the people of Korea.

I would like to express my sincere appreciation to Yi Hui-song, a writer of children's literature, who as my friend and teacher introduced me to Korean literature and encouraged me in my attempts at translation. She has given invaluable assistance in the painstaking task of checking the accuracy of my understanding of the original texts.

There is one distinct advantage in living and working over an extended period in the culture of the authors whose works are being translated. That can also even include an acquaintance with the authors themselves. It is not always that a translator has the privilege of personal acquaintance with an author. Choe Chong-hui, who has stories included here, helped me herself to choose which of her works to translate. She also assisted me in understanding more precisely the background of her stories. I feel especially grateful for all of her encouragement and support.

I owe much to my husband, a walking English thesaurus, without whose encouragement and assistance I would never have tried these translation from Korean literature.

I would also like to express my gratitude to The Si-sa-yong-o-sa Publishers, Inc., for making this collection available to the English-speaking world.

Genell Y. Poitras

Contents

Introduction

I

The Contemporary Korean Short Story — A Brief Survey

Much importance has been attached to the short story in contemporary Korea. Together with poetry, it has been regarded as a major literary genre by both serious readers and writers. An excellent short story will receive much critical applause while a number of popular novels go unnoticed simply because they are written for lowbrows. A writer devoted to the short story exclusively tends to flatter himself that he is a 'genuine and pure' writer free from the corrupting influence of commercialism, though there has been a growing impatience with this tendency in recent years. Much of what has been said is remarkable in that the short story has played a minor role on the literary scene in Europe and America. It is interesting in this connection to note that no distinction is usually made between a novel and a short story in common usage, though there are specific Korean terms for them. Consequently Korean students writing in English make no such distinction, and it is one of the most common English mistakes Korean students make.

The prestige the short story enjoys can safely be said to be one obvious feature of contemporary Korean literature. Perhaps we need not go far to seek the reason. The importance attached to the short story is almost entirely due to the peculiarity of the Korean literary market. An aspiring young writer on both sides of the Atlantic would send his work to a publisher and have it accepted or rejected. After a series of abortive attempts he might have his book published and awake one fine morning to find himself famous or underestimated. However, this is not the case with the Korean writer. To begin with, there would be no publisher daring enough to publish a book by an abscure author. Publishing even a book by a well-known writer of fiction frequently means financial loss, so that the role of discovering promising young writers is assigned to highbrow literary magazines. Some literary periodicals, monthly or quarterly, try to promote young writers by printing their works. Because of limited space, brief short stories are preferred and long works of novel size discouraged. So far as the preference for the short story is concerned, it applies also to well-known established authors.

Korea is one of the few countries in the world where the daily newspapers still make it a rule to print novels in serial form. The newspaper serial novel is intended for just as mixed a public as the radio drama, and it has every reason to cater to popular taste. The fondness for sentimentalism as well as for exaggeration, seductions, and acts of cruelty is among its chief characteristics. Naturally serious writers are reluctant to produce the 'lowbrow entertainments' called serials, though writers of the serials are fairly well paid. Writing serials is usually regarded as an artistic degradation or a loss of artistic integrity. And the 'novel' is almost synonymous with the 'newspaper serial' in Korea, hence the importance attached to the short story. Perhaps every artist, overwhelmed by the pressure of mass culture, nowadays finds himself in the painful situation of having to choose between being despised and despicable. Although a change has recently been noticeable, serious writers determined to refuse to be despicable have remained faithful to the short story.

So much for the short story itself. Kim Tong-in, Yom Sang-sop, Choe Hak-song, and Hyon Chin-gon were active as short story writers in the 1920s and early 1930s. Despite their ideological and temperamental differences, their works share deep humanitarian concern over the suffering and poverty of the oppressed people under the notorious Japanese colonial rule. Their stories are generally intended to be realistic accounts of events, behavior, and situations. It is significant that even Kim Tong-in, a harsh critic of tendencious literature with explicit political persuasions, should betray his overt sympathy for the persecuted Korean immigrants in Manchuria in his representative work *The Bare Hill* (Pulgun San). Apart from their literary merits, their works testify to the miserable living conditions of the Korean people in the early twentieth century.

They were soon joined by Yi Hyo-sok and Yu Chin-o, 'fellow travellers' and university wits, in the 1930s. After a brief period of flirtation with Socialist ideas, Yi and Yu turned out a number of short stories dealing with the dilemma of politically conscious and yet impotent intellectuals, the everyday life of the petty bourgeoisie, and falsely idyllic aspects of rural life. Both of them were writers of great attraction, but the promise never seems to have been fulfilled. Yi Hyo-sok's literary efforts came to a sudden end with his early death, and Yu Chin-o gave up writing for a university career.

The contemporary Korean short story, so to speak, came of age with Kim Yu-jong, Yi Sang, Kim Tong-ni, and Hwang Sun-won who began to be active in the late 1930s onwards. With the exception of Yi Sang, each of them came of Lower middle-class rural families. Their stories at their best are concerned with rural peasants driven to hard work and penury. The stories are told with detachment, often with a sense of humor in an ironic vein. A touch of pathos runs deep, but you can find neither exaggeration nor false sentimentalism in their stories. Readers of the stories are often left with the feeling that they have become freshly acquainted with what is really indigenous to Korea. Each of these writers is a unique stylist in his own way, and their stylistic efforts have exerted a great influence upon the younger writers coming after them. Kim Tong-ni and Hwang Sun-won have also tried their hand at the novel, but their novels have never attained the heights reached by their short stories.

Korea's liberation from Japanese rule marked a new era in literature as in other fields. Poets and writers enjoyed freedom of expression to an unprecedented degree. However, the period of complete freedom did not last long, and the worst trial was in store for them. The outbreak of the Korean War in 1950 drove them to utter despair, and it took them a long time to recover from the trauma. Stories dealing with man's inhumanity to man during the war and battlefield experiences flooded in. The inability to recount a story with detachment, or 'aesthetic distance', as well as the restricted freedom of expression leaves a number of documentary stories tasteless. Ha Kun-chan, Yi Ho-chol, So Ki-won, and Sonu Hwi may be cited as representative writers of the post-war school.

A group of gifted writers emerged in the 1960s and 1970s. Active and prolific, they have turned out a great number of stories about the dehumanizing effects of modernization and industrialization. Alienated, frustrated, and unhappy figures people their stories. Their stories are too dissimilar in subject and tone for a neat generalization. On the whole, however, they share a belief in the liberating and enlightening role of literature, and we can characterize their stories as realistic in the sense that realism means the objective representation of contemporary social reality. Hwang Sok-yong, Yi Mun-gu, Yi Chong-jun, Kim Sung-ok, and Cho Son-jak are major writers of the group of the 1960s and 1970s. As most of them are still young, in what direction they will develop remains to be seen.

II

Many contemporary Korean authors write about people in everyday situations who view their roles in life as being subject to a kind of inevitable destiny. The ease with which ordinary happenings are ascribed to fate in that context is difficult for the Western mind to comprehend. In addition, there is sometimes a tendency to romanticize the life of the poor in Korean literature, and even to endow the unfortunate with higher morals, sometimes just because of their poverty. Choe Chong-hui does not, however, succumb to that temptation. Rather, her characters are presented with warts and all, giving her works a much greater authenticity.

The stories in this small volume might be compared to the Flemish painters of Bruegel's time. A close look at Bruegel's paintings, "The Peasant Wedding" or "The Harvesters," or "The Peasant Dance," reveals a vivid picture of the humor and character of the common people of 16th century Flanders. The stories by Choi Chong-hui and Pak Yong-jun paint this kind of a picture of village life in Korea.

Choi Chong-hui, Hwang Sun-won and Pak Yong-jun belong to the same generation of literary figures, the senior generation born shortly after 1910, who lived through both world wars under the domination of Japan.

Choe Chong-hui was born in 1912 in the province of North Ham-gyong, which is now in the eastern part of north Korea. She was the eldest of four children. In 1924 the family moved to Seoul, where she attended high school. After graduation from a school for the training of kindergarten teachers she spent a few months teaching in one of the Southern provinces and then a year in Japan. Choe has lived most of her adult life in the capital city of Seoul, with the exception of seven years in Tokyo and the two years of refugee life in Taegu. She still continues to write.

Choe dates the writing of this novel as having been written from 1947 to 1958. The two short stories, "Chom-nye" and "The Ritual at the Well," were published in 1946 and "Round and Round the Pagoda" came out in 1976.

Her literary debut was in 1935 with the publication of the short story, "Hyung-ga" in the literary magazine, *Cho-gwang*. She had just been released from a year in prison, having been taken into custody by the Japanese for having been implicated in the "Shin Kon Sol" case although she was not herself a member of the group which went by that name. Upon her release she began work at the *Chosun Ilbo*, a daily newspaper in Seoul, in the publications department.

It was in 1937 that she and her husband, the poet Kim Tong-whan whose pen name is Pa-in, moved to the small farming village of Tokso, east of Seoul, in order to escape the constant surveillance of the Japanese. It seems ironical that later he was accussed of having cooperated with the Japanese and put in prison under the anti-government laws. The period from 1945 until the outbreak of the Korean War on June 25, 1950, when Korea was attempting to establish a government of its own, was a period of inner strife, unrest and suspicion. Then, after the invasion Pa-in was again under suspicion but this time for being a communist sympathizer. Finally, in order to save his family further harassment, he turned himself in shortly after June 25, 1950 and was never seen or heard from again.

Choe has the unusual ability of portraying the most devastating circumstances with a great deal of humor. The trip to Tokso at night with the baby and her old mother on top of the truck piled high with their freight, only to arrive and find that Pa-in had asked an old man to meet them evokes laughter, not tears. She is painfully honest about her own feelings and does not try to make herself appear in a favorable light. The scene of her having had too much to drink and then ranting and raving is a good example of this utter honesty on her part. She does not try to pretend that she is not frightened or upset. She also is honest about the way in which people easily take advantage of her.

Perhaps the most poignant scene in the whole story is the flight from Seoul, when Choe Chong-hui tries to keep the small form of her daughter on the truck ahead in view. When she eventually loses sight of A-ran we are caught up in her uneasiness as to what will happen, and since this is a true story we know that the daughter might well never be found.

Introduction

There are numerous books about the Korean War, analyses of how the war came about and other theoretical studies, for example, about how the division of Korea might have been avoided. This novel by Choe helps to provide an ingredient missing from most of these theoretical or objective historical accounts, in that it gives a vivid picture of those other than military personnel who were caught by the invasion and who fled from Seoul to cities in the south. The uncertainties produced by the dilemmas of whether to leave and where to go are made very real. Now and then there are characters who in the confusion of flight are able to help a lost child, for example, the unknown truck drive in Yong Dong who finds Choe's daughter, A-ran wandering in the streets alone and takes her to the home of the police chief in that town.

It would have been easy for Choe to paint Pa-in as the model husband. But with a great amount of humor she is able to depict him not only as a sensitive man, a father who enjoys his children but also as an awkward and sometimes overly sentimental person.

Choe has from the beginning of her literary career persisted in writing about the traditions which bind and control the lives of women in a male dominated society.

The literary critic, Cho Pyong-bu, in his introduction to a collection of her short stories published in 1976, says that there are few authors like Choe who continue to write about women and the traditions that so completely control them. He reiterates that in his opinion there is no other author who has so relentlessly pursued the world of women as Choe Chong-hui. She is recognized as one of Korea's leading woman authors.

The scenes of village life in Korea, so vividly portrayed in "The Ritual at the Well" and "Chom-nye," might be compared with some of the paintings of village life by the Flemish painters. A close look at Bruegel's paintings "The Peasant Wedding," "The Harvesters," or "The Peasant Dance," discloses a vivid picture of the humor and character of the common people of 16th century Flanders. The two stories mentioned above paint this kind of a picture of village life in Korea. As in Bruegel's paintings the common people do not "dress-up" to have their picture painted. So, too, in Choe's stories the reader is allowed to see life as it actually is. Her description of the meaning of starvation, the need to pick the greens on the hillside in early spring because there is nothing else to eat, and the result of eating only greens in the diet are portrayed with simplicity and clarity. In her scenes nothing is left out in describing the fate of the poor.

For centuries, and even well into the twentieth century, there has existed a class system in Korea, the nobility called the *yangban* and the commoner the *sangnom*. The landlords in "Chom-nye" and "The Ritual at the Well" belonged to the *yangban*, or privileged class, whereas the tenants were the *sangnom*. There was no way of changing their status. It was their fate.

As mentioned previously, Choe has pursued the theme of women in a male dominated society in her works. Into this theme she weaves the contrast between the rich and the poor, most clearly exemplified in the power and control of the landlord over his tenants. The importance of spirit worship which binds the poor people to dependence on fortune-tellers, of observances to placate spirits, and of control by the *mudang* is clearly portrayed in the two stories, "Chom-nye" and "The Ritual at the Well."

Choe does not attempt to compel the reader to identify with the plight of the poor by endowing them with kind and generous characters. Instead she presents them honestly as humans, capable of jealousy and lack of sympathy, and impressed by wealth. Even the *mudang*, of the same social class as Chom-nye's family, is sly and heartless, taking all of Chom-nye's clothing and the one remaining chicken.

In Poryon-wha, the main character in "Round and Round the Pagoda," Choe creates one of these women bound by the traditions of centuries, who through four generations of adversity obediently accepts her fate. In the end she dies peacefully, having resolved the final conflict with her great-granddaughter. She still continues to believe that the two Koreas will be unified and that her son and grandson will return.

Hwang Sun-won, one of Korea's best-known and prolific writers, made his literary debut at the age of 15 with the publishing of a children's story and poetry in a daily newspaper. His first volume of short stories appeared in 1940. This story is a sensitive approach to the maturation process of a child as seen symbolically through the life of a crab.

Pak Yong-jun published his first short stories in 1934 at the age of 22. "The Touch of Life" came out in 1955. He is the only author in this collection who is no longer living. The struggles of Chong-hae in this story as he gradually alienates himself from his family and fellow teachers could be set in any culture. This story recognizes that people do not exist in a vacuum entirely independent of others. In order to find fulfillment as human beings, all must be able to accept sympathy, to cry and laugh together with others.

My hope is that this brief selection of short stories depicting life in Korea will encourage a deeper interest in contemporary Korean literature.

G.Y.P.

THE CRUEL CITY
and Other Korean Short Stories

The Cruel City

by Yi Chong-jun
translated by Choe Yong

1

As the chilly dusk of autumn settled over the prison grounds, a small, shriveled-up old man suddenly appeared and walked down the path away from the prison. This seldom occurred nowadays. The prison was located at the northwestern corner of the city by the park woods, where the cherry trees and alders were planted at random. Near the entrance of this park, where the man-made woods ended, a path of about 200 meters led to the prison. From the park entrance one could look down at the prison grounds and see the path and the tall gloomy buildings of the prison compound as if it were one's own palm. Even a dog's movement couldn't be missed if it moved up or down the prison path.

However, there had been no movement for a long time which could draw one's attention. One seldom saw anyone with business at the prison going up or down the path. Those freed from the prison were much fewer than those newly put into the prison. Though the flow of those entering the prison never ceased, these convicts were always transported inside by a wire-windowed bus. Of course, the prison officers and people living in the area used the path. But their movement did not draw any special attention. The movements which drew attention on this path would be those of prisoners who had either finished their terms or were paroled by the authorities.

Though no one knew why, within the last couple of years no inmate had been freed. The prison gate had not opened once to free an inmate. Some doubted whether there were any prisoners at all in the prison; others thought the prison only accommodated those who were serving life terms. Almost no one could remember when the last prisoner walked out of that prison. Even among the officials of the prison, perhaps, few had a clear memory of the last time they opened the iron gate to send a lucky inmate into the outer world.

The inmates were not the only ones who were not seen any more. The path to the prison had been frequented for a while by visitors. But they too had disappeared completely, though from when, no one knew.

The prison path became a deserted road, long lost in the stillness. The existence of the prison and its inmates was absolutely forgotten in the outside world.

Nonetheless, the prison employees continued to do their jobs, and every night, without exception, the searchlights on the high watchtowers resumed their tireless duties. They alone were the unmistakable proof that the prison still functioned amidst the deep oblivion of the world. As if to prove this, a man at last appeared on the path one evening. The prison was not an empty, haunted shell after all, or a place inhabited only by "lifers." The fact that a man walked onto the prison pathway testified to this.

The sudden release of a prisoner had not happened in a long time, and accordingly it drew one's attention. There was, however, no sign of either sentimental remembrance or joy on the face of this man. He moved slowly and monotonously. He carried a small, worn-out package containing his personal belongings. It was the property he had left with the prison officials so many years ago and it was all he had in the world. The dyed field jacket he wore, of a fashion popular after the Korean War, was as worn out and as faded as the man. The trousers, too, were worn and plain. The grey hair was unkempt. The attire matched the man's mood and hinted at the amount of time he had spent in his cell, beyond of the oblivion of the world outside.

The man was, of course, alone. He was accompanied neither by fellow inmates nor met by relatives. His shadow, elongated by evening twilight settling over the forest, was his only company. He was walking toward the setting sun so his shadow was drawn long behind him. His legs drew heavy steps, as if carrying his shadow on his shoulders after pulling it out of prison. Occasionally, he slowed his pace and twitched his nose slightly as if his eyes could not adjust to the autumnal twilight. He seemed to be having difficulty carrying his shadow down the prison path. Only when the weakened sunlight hindered his vision did the man show any change in his expression or his gait. Perhaps troubled, he continued slowly walking down the path away from the prison. After walking the length of the path, he reached the entrance to the park and his expression changed. A sign announced: "The birds are longing for sky and forest."

A small store was located at the park entrance on the right side. Hanging on the branches of the cherry trees around the store were bird cages—some small, some large—and several placards proclaiming:

"Your merciful release of the captive birds will be rewarded with your own freedom!"

"Grant freedom to the birds!"

The store sold the birds to customers who would then release them as a sort of offering for their own independence. The man stopped in front of the store as if he had emerged from a long tunnel at last. With a deep sense of security, the man nodded a couple of times and something like a smile spread over his dry, worn-out face. He glanced over his shoulder back down the length of the path towards the prison, and walked across the street to the bird store.

The proprietor of the store was just concluding a deal with a middle-aged man.

"Sir, when you give this little fellow the freedom to fly over the forest, it's just like buying your own lifelong independence. . . ."

The salesman was about thirty with a sharply pointed chin and white, steel-framed glasses behind which his eyes darted alertly. He seemed arrogant and stingy even as he handed a bird cage over to his customer.

"Now open the cage door and let this bird fly like it was meant to. You'll be fully repaid for today's charity, sir."

In contrast to the aggressive assurance of the salesman, the customer reluctantly received the bird cage. The old man approached the scene cautiously so as not to disturb the transaction by his abrupt appearance. Neither the salesman nor his customer noticed the old man, anyway. They took no interest in such shabbily dressed old-timer.

The old man could conceal his curiosity no longer. The distance between the two men and him shortened with each step. He moved like a child carefully peeking into an adult's world, or an urchin who was unable to contain his interest any longer. He watched the customer closely, afraid that the interesting scene would stop if the middle-aged man changed his mind.

"Fly! Don't forget me when you're flying overhead free from your cage."

Having reminded the bird of his charity, the middle-aged man opened the cage door wide. But the bird in the cage didn't seem to understand what was going on around him. He nodded a couple of times and, finally, with a puzzled look, seemed to comprehend the situation. He left the cage at last, leaving behind a slight fluttering sound.

The bird seemed to show off its style for a while, flying high in the twilit sky. Suddenly, he became a black spot in the sky and disappeared into the woods.

"He's flying nicely," said the bird's middle-aged liberator with satisfaction, when the bird had vanished completely from the sight. Then he left the store with light steps, as if he himself had invisible wings.

The old man stood there motionless even after the middle-aged man had left. For a long time he fixed his eyes on the sky where the bird had disappeared. He was not conscious of the middle-aged man's departure. He was more deeply touched by the fact that the bird was released than that the middle-aged man had been the one to pay for it. In fact the old man caught his breath and with innocent joy and suppressed excitement, had watched the bird soaring into the sky. And with the joy and excitement was a certain look of envy. For some time the old man stood transfixed watching the sky where the bird had flown off. The old man could not get rid of the envy in his heart, an envy that could be either for the bird now soaring in the sky or for the middle-aged man who had granted it freedom. No matter what, the old man was enjoying himself more than the man who released the bird.

The man finally stopped looking at the sky, and already his eyes expressed a deep sense of loss. The middle-aged man went into the park, and the salesman disappeared into the store. The old man looked embarrassed, hesitating as to what to do next. Left alone in front of the store, he had nothing to do. But, like one caught in a trap, he could not leave. He lingered around the store as if waiting for another transaction to take place. He was loitering, hoping something would happen. He seemed to be having difficulty deciding something. He made a movement, and then turned abruptly away from the store. He then reversed himself, going away from and then back to the store alternately. No one else who passed by showed any interest in the store. When the young man who minded the store emerged, the old man's anxious face brightened with the expectation that something would happen soon. In spite of himself, he moved nearer the store yet again. The young man, by contrast, seemed indifferent to this shabby and withered old man. He had come out to close the shop. The old man was perplexed when he saw the salesman carry one by one the bird cages into the shop.

"Are you closing the store?" The old man hurriedly approached the shop despite himself.

"Yes, it's getting dark." The young man hardly glanced at him and this unconcern appeared to help the old man reach a decision.

"Well, then. . . ." The old man said, as if to gain the younger's attention and compelled him to stop carrying the cages inside for a moment. The young man did indeed stop his work, and turned to face the old man.

"Do you have any business with me. . . ?" he asked impatiently. He had just decided to close for the day and seemed to be rebuking the old man for this troublesome interruption. The salesman's tone caused the old man's decision to waver.

"No,. . . I. . . I. . . Just. . . ." The old man mumbled as if he had said the wrong thing. His hands, which had been fumbling in his trouser pocket, ceased their motion. The young man turned away, and resumed taking the cages down and carrying them into the store.

The old man simply stood and watched the young man's activity. Soon the young man disappeared inside the shop and the loneliness descended upon the old man. He looked at the shop door and presently nodded at it, as if he had at last made a resolution. Next, he yawned and walked towards the park woods, disappearing himself into the dark forest shadows.

2

Bright morning sunshine, flooded the trees with light and bird sounds, filled the air around the park the next morning. The chill of autumn wavered. The old man, with his bundle of possessions under his arm, wandered the park amidst the light and bird sounds. As leisurely as an old man from the neighborhood out for a morning stroll and as attentively as the groundkeeper, he looked in every corner of the park, searching around the benches and in the sandbox in the playground. It was clear that the old man was neither strolling around the park nor scavenging the park. He picked up cigarette butts, and every so often he came upon a coin under a bench or in the sandbox. His eyes were extraordinarily sharp and motions in contrast excessively pliable. He never missed a cigarette butt underfoot in a good condition. Neither a single coin scattered under the benches or in the sandbox escaped his sharp eyes no matter how well-hidden. He searched every corner of the park for butts and coins. He kept the two collections carefully separated in the two pockets of his dyed army jacket, cigarettes in the right pocket and coins in the left pocket. Once he picked up very skillfully a coin hidden under the earth hardened by frequented footsteps. His pilgrimage around the park continued until he came to the park entrance, by which time the sun had risen high upward in the eastern sky. His left pocket, filled with coins, had gained considerably in weight. With his hand tucked in this pocket, he made for the park entrance, thinking to satisfy his appetite. But at the moment of getting out of the park the old man was again interrupted.

The bird shop was open already, and the young owner seemed very busy with his morning affairs. A crowd of customers stood in front of the bird cages hanging from the trees. A look of curiosity came to the old man's face. "Even this early in the morning the customers come. . . ."

The old man forgot his empty stomach and approached the

store warily. As if it were a mysterious ritual he watched the bargaining between the salesman and the customers. From early morning, the bird business thrived. The people jammed in front of the store were not just browsers. They were really buying the birds and rejoicing in their release. The purchasers did not seem solemn. They light-heartedly paid for the birds and let them fly off. It was a carefree pastime, and 200 won was cheap for such entertainment. The old man who was carefully watching the scene was the one who most experienced the pleasure of buying and the joy of the birds' flight. When a customer opened a bird cage and let the inhabitant fly off, the old man looked on like a child lost in envy at the trail of the released bird.

As the day passed the young owner's business continued to pick up. The customers kept coming. Some who dropped in bought the birds quickly without a second thought. The birds sold continually so the old man hardly left the area of the store. He took a place under a tree across from the shop and sat on the ground, forgetting entirely his thoughts of breakfast.

Not until the store emptied of customers, its peak hours of operation apparently over, did the old man ventured to speak to the shop owner. He took out a cigarette butt from his army jacket and put it to his mouth. "Your bird business is doing very well, young man. . . ."

The man with the pointed chin and white metal-framed glasses showed no sign of interest in the old man, however. He hadn't even noticed that the old man had reappeared. But the old man seemed unconcerned with the young man's attitude.

"In the old days, the people who bought wings were different from your customers. Quite different." The old man went on as if reciting a soliloquy. He didn't seem to care whether the young man was listening or not. Abruptly, the shopkeeper felt ill at ease about the old man. He glanced at him furtively, and his face changed expression for a moment when he recognized this old man as the one who had appeared at the store the day before. He seemed annoyed at the old man's reappearance.

"Yes, that's true. In those days only visitors for the prison used to buy birds. Nowadays, there are hardly any visitors." The young man spoke impatiently as if his intention was to drive the old man away. His words implied that none of this was the old man's business.

But in spite of the young man's arrogant tone, the old man's face brightened. "Of course, it doesn't matter to you what kind of people the customers are. If they buy the birds, you'll be satisfied. But you seem to have been in this business for some time since you know about the visitors to the prison. You must have set up shop some time ago. . . ."

The young man looked the old man over carefully. The old man's words struck the younger man as peculiar.

"I've been in business here for about ten years. How do you know all about this?" he asked the old man. He had by now figured out who the old man was from his appearance. The young man's tone became polite and cautious.

"I frequented this place long before you began your business. You remember at most the days when visitors to the prison were your customers. But before then it was the prisoners who had just been released that bought the birds. Even then, not many prisoners were released, so there were few such customers. Perhaps one man every two or three days. . . at most about ten men a week passed by here when they were released from prison. With only the ex-convicts as customers, the business hardly thrived. But if the number of people who purchased the birds was fewer, the price for the birds was much higher. The privilege of releasing a bird cost a prisoner about half a year's wages."

The salesman listened without comment. The old man's expression and the tone of his voice grew more excited. He continued with feeling.

"Anyway, in those days everyone who came out of the prison bought a bird at this store. This money, mind you, was earned by the sweat of his brow while in prison. Though some ex-cons relied on their families to pay for a bird, most of the released prisoners eagerly spent the wages of months of toil. None of them regretted it, or ever missed the money."

". . . . ."

"Yes, there were few customers in those days. The store was not as big as this one. Originally, it was an old man who was released from the prison who started the business. There were only a few bird cages hanging from the trees then. This old man had a young grandson of about 14 years old who later kept the store. Even then there was no real building erected, and no placards either. The times were bad. The salesman just hung up the cages on the trees and waited for a released prisoner to come by. And the prisoners became fewer and fewer. And the clientele changed from the convicts themselves to those who used to visit them."

". . . . ."

"Now even these visitors have ceased coming. Since you remember those days, you must have first come to the store around then. When I last saw this place, the original owner's grandson, now in his twenties, was still minding the store. If you've been in charge here since about then, you've probably worked here for about ten years. But. . . ."

The old man's voice lost its enthusiasm and suddenly became dispirited; the young man was not listening any more. The young man was waiting on a customer, concealing his interest in the old man's narrative under a mask of weariness. The old man kept quiet. He was not easily disappointed, so he took a new interest in the bargaining between the salesman and his new customer. Presently, the customer bought a bird, let it fly away, and then left the store. Though the old man waited patiently for the young man to pay attention to him, the young man continued to ignore him. Both the old man and the young man seemed to be waiting for a customer, but the morning business had apparently already peaked; not a single customer came to the store after the most recent one had left. Suffocating and tedious moments passed, and it seemed that the old man endured the passage of time less easily than the young man. Several times the old man fiddled with the coins in his left pocket. And after several false starts, indecisively, the old man could no longer endure the pressure and he pushed himself toward the young man.

"Now, then, show me a bird, too." In his outstretched hand was a collection of soiled coins. Uncomprehendingly, the young man looked at the old man.

"Probably, this money is not enough to purchase a bird. Give me a twenty-won discount and sell me the bird."

The old man counted the coins, moving them from one hand to the other. There were eighteen ten-won pieces, as the man had said. He poured the coins on the store counter and implored the salesman. "Come now. . . . in fact, I've been waiting to do this since yesterday."

The young man didn't answer, but he seemed to understand the old man. He pointed to a bird cage without saying anything. Relieved, the old man approached the cage and looked into it for a while as if trying to get acquainted with the bird, or perhaps savoring the moments before he would liberate it. With sudden decision, he opened the cage door. The bird, tiny and cute, escaped from the cage after rolling his eyes around in a quick motion. The old man's face was one big smile as he watched the bird fly to the park woods. His open mouth showed yellow teeth long after the bird had disappeared out of sight.

"If I am correct, you were. . . ." This time it was the young man who initiated the conversation. Was it because the old man's behavior worried him? "You were probably released from the prison yesterday, weren't you?"

The old man seemed embarrassed by the young man's sudden intimacy. He answered quickly, as if afraid of losing the young man's attention. "That's right. Yesterday. Just yesterday I came out of that jail. Then I came straight over here." He talked as if to prove it to himself. But in contrast to the old man's hasty speech, the young man was cool and businesslike.

"You came out of prison yesterday. . . . That's very unusual. You must have been there quite some time—maybe ten or fifteen years?"

"Well, I can't count all the years I've spent there. This time alone I was in for more than twelve years."

"So you've been there before?"

"Yes, indeed. I've spent almost all my life there. I'd no sooner be released than I'd find myself back again. The place is like a home to me!" Encouraged by the young man's interest, the old man seemed almost proud of himself.

"What were you in for all those times?"

"I can't figure it out myself. I'd just find myself back in. It became a sort of habit. . . Once you spend enough time there, it begins to seem like home. . . From the beginning I got the feeling that my life won't be smoothly worked out. The first conviction was right after I returned from sea. I took a rough fishing job so I could feed my wife and children. When I returned home, I found out that my wife had been sleeping with another man. I tried to kill them both. No one forgives an adulterous wife. To make matters worse, the man used to be a cop, a flunkey for the Japanese during the Japanese occupation. . . . Anyway neither of them was killed and I wound up in prison. It doesn't make any sense to dwell on the past, but with a start like that, jail got to be a habit, as if I were caught in a trap. I actually prowled around the prison grounds before eventually returning back inside. . . ." The old man spoke with animation. The young salesman was persuaded that he was telling the truth.

"So, that's the story. And that's why you've been here like this since you came out of prison yesterday." The young man asked this cautiously as if only to confirm what he had deduced. But the old man missed the meaning of the question.

" 'Like this?' What do you mean by saying 'like this?' " he shot back impatiently.

"What I meant was that there's a reason for you lingering around this area. Shouldn't a free man be eager to get back to his relatives as soon as possible? But maybe you don't have a family to go back to." The young man expressed this last sentiment in a cool, impassive voice.

But the old man's reply was unexpectedly sharp. "I do so have a family. How dare you say I have no place to go?" The old man spoke defiantly. "It's not true that I am without a home and family. My family is very well-off. I'm just waiting for my son."

"A son? So you're waiting for your son?"

"Of course. My son is back at home. As decent fellow as you are. He owns a house—a fine, spacious roof-tiled house fenced with tall citrus trees. In the back yard bamboo trees grow thick. It's a country house so the garden is very big. My son owns the house, but I feel like it's my home."

There was a note of desperation in the old man's voice. The salesman maintained his air of indifference.

"Then why are you waiting here for your son instead of immediately running to that nice house?" The young man now wore a faint smile. By contrast, the old man's tone got more sincere.

"I don't want to pass him on the road. I've already notified him of the date of my release in a letter."

"Then why hasn't your son come up to meet you on the day of your release, if he knew the date?"

"The letter was probably delayed. But once he gets it, he'll rush here to me. That's why I'm waiting here — so we don't miss each other on the road. If he finds out that I've already left, he'll be sorely disappointed. Without him, I wouldn't have any reason to get out of prison." The old man asserted his son's filial affection with strong confidence. The young man did not seem persuaded.

"Well, I think it'll take him some time to get here. But you can't do anything about that now. If your son ever does appear. . . if you believe he'll show, then you'll have to wait here for him." The young man looked as if he were suppressing a smile, but the old man seemed not to notice.

"Yes, of course, I've got to wait. I'll wait until he shows up. In the meantime, I have something to do here."

"What else do you have to do here except to wait for your son?" the young man asked jokingly.

"I have things to do here. Even if my son showed up right now, I couldn't leave without finishing what I've got to do. I have to spend several days here, so my son's delay actually helps the situation."

"And what business would be more important than your son's arrival?"

"You wouldn't understand if I explained to you. Let's not discuss this further—it's better not to hear what you can't comprehend. You can be satisfied with thinking that I'm just lingering around waiting for my son."

The young man made no reply.

"I think I'm pretty lucky to have such a son. You know that many prisoners prefer to stay in jail until they become jail ghost because they have no family on the outside and no place to go. Compared to them, I'm fortunate, yes. . . ." The old man continued to assure himself that he was fortunate, but the young man was no longer listening. A customer had entered the store and the young man's attention was focused on him. The old man shut his mouth, and soon became absorbed in the transaction taking place in the store.

3

Perhaps it was true that the old man was waiting for his son to come to him. He seemed trapped in the park, like the birds in their cages. He seemed held to the spot.

As he had the day before, the old man walked through the chilly morning air in the woods the next morning. He resumed his chores of the day before, searching for cigarette butts and coins on the sidewalks and under the benches. By the time he reached the park entrance after passing through the paths in the woods and by the sandbox in the playground, the morning sun was high in the eastern sky just like the day before. There was no sign of hesitation now as he approached the bird store. Through the park entrance, the old man walked directly towards it.

The store, of course, had been open since early in the morning and the young salesman was busy with the customers who filled his shop. He didn't have time for so much as a glance at the old man. The old man was in no hurry. He calmly took a seat beside a tree near the store and watched the day's transactions. As each deal was concluded, the old man watched the bird for a long time, more concerned than any of the customers. As noon approached it was clear that business was slacking off a bit. Then the old man seemed to reach for his own pleasure instead of vicariously enjoying that of others. Able to contain himself no longer, he got up to buy a bird with the coins he had collected in the park.

"Here's the money. Give me one of those birds. . . . I'm just a little short. . . ."

The old man pushed forward a handful of coins and put on an expression that was both shameless and imploring, like a drug addict who didn't have enough cash for a fix. The young salesman met this expression with a look of blank dismay. After counting the coins one by one, the old man handed them over to the storekeeper. He concluded the bargain by himself. He lifted down the cage that the young man had indicated and released the bird with a tender, cautious motion.

The old man stared over the park woods where the bird had flown, his eyes expressing a pained sense of loss. At that very moment, the young man, his own eyes full of pity, began to speak in a tone unfit for a merchant.

"I can't understand why you're doing such a useless thing."

The old man turned, an awkward smile on his face, as if he had just been caught at some stupid deed. "Well, that's what I wanted to do. . . whenever I came out of jail I used to do this. . . ."

"But you already bought a bird yesterday, didn't you?" The young man pressed the point contemptuously, though his attitude was covered by a polite tone. The old man welcomed even this response, and his voice became more and more elated.

"Oh, yes. But that was for myself. This bird isn't for me. It's for Mr. Song."

"Mr. Song?"

"A friend of mine, a cellmate. He was a mayor before they put him into jail. He used to brag a lot about the good old days, and say that once he got out of jail he'd live a decent life in a house. . . money. . . ."

"Then why are you paying for a bird on his behalf?"

"That's because he was so much more eager about buying one than the other inmates. Most inmates look forward to buying a bird, but he was really counting the days until he could do it. That Mr. Song was extraordinarily concerned about releasing a bird. But he couldn't make it. So I did it for him."

"Are they still talking about releasing birds in the prison?"

"Of course. We've all done it before, which is why we're talking about it and waiting for the day when we can do it again. Most of us say that we're not buying birds, but 'wings'."

"Since there are so many inmates who look forward to buying birds, how come no one's ever released? Why can't they come out like you?" The young man's question was preposterous—as if it were up to the inmates themselves whether they could get out of prison. But the old man took the stupid question seriously.

"Perhaps. . . ." The old man put a serious expression on his face as if he knew the answer. "Perhaps it's because there's some communications problem. Some of our letters don't seem to reach home. When our terms are about half over, we generally take an interest in writing. As you know, most of us have families in our hometowns. You can imagine how much we boast about our families and hometowns while in prison.

Please come to greet me. I'm almost finished with my sentence, so be prepared to meet me.' If one of us wrote these lines, how proud he was—and how the others envied him."

"So you all keep in close touch with your families?"

After a long interval the old man shook his head slowly and replied dejectedly to the young man's question. "No, we don't."

"You don't?"

"None of us really thinks things out. We don't care much about the replies."

"Hasn't anyone ever been paroled through the offices of his family?"

"No."

"But you do receive visitors, and get letters in the mail?"

"No, neither. No family visits, no letters. But we never talk about it. Despite this, no one mentions the letters home. We don't regard them as lies. It's not necessary to talk about them, so no one regards them as lies."

The old man continued. "But we assume one thing: that our letters have never reached our families. You might not believe this, but that's what happened. So our families forget about us."

"But you did write to your son? And you were lucky enough to get in touch with him and to get out of prison, weren't you?"

The young man had asked this in a concerned voice, but the old man had become more depressed. He shook his head feebly. "No, though I've written him frequently, my letters haven't seemed to reach him yet."

"Did your release have anything to do with your son?"

"Well, my term is not completely finished. I got paroled before I heard from my son. But it was all due to him. I couldn't have gotten out of that place if I didn't have a son and a home to go to. I am so eager to see my son and grandsons, and also that house. For so long I've dreamt about my son and his house. The house—surrounded by citrus trees and with a spacious garden, basking in sunlight. . . .Anyway, I've decided to meet my son even though I didn't get in touch with him. . . ." When he talked about his son and his home again, the old man cheered up. He paused, as if indulging himself in a memory of the place, and then continued speaking.

"Eventually, my faith in him made me get out of prison. The other inmates didn't have my faith, nor my intense longing for a home. That's why they didn't dare come out of jail. But now I can see my son and perhaps he will be very sorry for letting his father be released in this fashion. . . ."

"Then you're to wait for him without any definite plan, since your son was not notified of your release?" The cold contemptuous expression had reappeared on the face of the young man.

"I can't wait for him here forever, of course. If he doesn't show up eventually, then I'll go out to find him. . . . But in the meantime, I should wait for him. The letter might reach him in a couple of days. And how deeply disappointed he'll be to have missed me."

"So are you just going to keep on buying birds for your friends in the jail?" The young man was practically jeering at him. A sneer appeared on his smooth face.

The old man was cornered and had to prepare answers. Now he was at a loss and unable to make a reply. With a discouraged tone, he haltingly gave a vague answer.

"If I can, then why not? Those guys are very anxious to buy 'wings'."

The young man mocked the old man. "Oh, you will, will you? Until your obedient son appears to meet you. . . ."

The old man finally shut up. For some reason the young man seemed to be angry with him. For a while, the old man studied the young man's features, thinking maybe that he himself was to blame for this outburst. But he was unable to affect the young man's mood. He left the store despondently, as if he recognized that there was no help for it except the passing of time.

4

When the old man came back to the store it was almost sunset. He looked happier than before. He had been searching the park woods yet again, and his left pocket was heavy with the coins he had picked up for the next day. He put his hand in his pocket, as if confident that he could change the young man's mood with the coins.

He was going to buy another bird. He had already implied to the young man that he was going to continue buying birds for his friends in prison. He also wanted to please the young man who was selling the birds. The old man had nothing to do but buy birds anyway.

He figured to please the young man, but his timing was off. When he reached the store, a gentleman was quarrelling with the young man.

"I didn't sell you this bird at all, you should understand. I only sold you the right to release this bird into the woods. You absolutely cannot take this bird with you." The young man was eagerly explaining this to the gentleman. But the customer wouldn't give in an inch.

"I didn't say that I bought the bird itself, and I don't have any intention of keeping it at home. What I want to do is to release this bird at home with my children. And that's none of your business. Why should it matter to you if I release it here or at my home?"

The argument had started when the customer insisted on bringing the bird home to release it there, and the storekeeper wouldn't allow it. The dispute had been going on quite a while.

"Once you've purchased the bird, I don't care where you release it. But I can't trust you. How do I know whether you're going to release it or not? To tell the truth, I think you may want to keep this bird at home."

The gentleman lost his patience when the young man concluded in such a provoking and condescending way. "You should watch your mouth, young man. Do I look like a man who's going to keep this sparrow at home? And once I've paid for it, you've no right to meddle in this matter." The customer couldn't conceal his agitation. By contrast, the young proprietor was speaking in a calm, polite, easygoing manner.

"That's not quite so, sir"

"What do you mean by that?"

"I'm selling my customers the privilege of freeing the birds, not the right to keep them confined. I care that much about my birds."

"Freedom for his birds. . . that's an especially commendable thing for a bird salesman to say. So you keep the birds in a cage to protect their freedom?"

"That's because we humans can appreciate our freedom more meaningfully through the birds. But we can't restrain the birds—they should be released here."

"That's a very moving sentiment."

The gentleman responded with a surprised look. It didn't mean that he was persuaded by the young man's speech. He was indeed sneering at the storekeeper in his own way.

The old man thought that he had finally found an opening. He had a golden opportunity to prove his goodwill towards the young man because of this unexpected quarrelling.

"Yes, it is." The old man broke in for he could wait no longer. "This young man is right. Though it is none of my business I believe the truth wins out in the long run."

Both the customer and the young man were surprised at this abrupt interference, and each watched the old man in silence. The old man continued speaking quickly.

"To be frank, there are many people in the world who prefer keeping birds in a cage to letting them go wherever they want. I don't mean that you're one of them. You seem to be a man. It was busy searching around forest far away from him. The birds caught by the light was scattering around in the darkness like autumn leaves. It seemed there was almost man of his word. But for his part, the young man has made it all clear. He is providing his birds with wings. It's a matter of record that this man wants to watch his birds gain their freedom. And to make sure of this it's much wiser for him not to allow the birds to be taken away from here, whether he believes his customers or not."

The old man had reproached the gentleman with a grave expression but a mild tone. The customer looked amazed. The storekeeper was looking at the sky with nothing to say.

"Gads, what nonsense was it that led me to hear such a ridiculous speech. All right, then!" The customer, who was scrutinizing the old man with a questioning glance, was likely to retreat.

"I guess it'll be all right if I won't buy this bird. Isn't it true, young man? Now you refund me." The customer tapped on the young man's shoulder jokingly. Then the young salesman also waited upon the customer in a friendly manner as if they mutually understood.

"Then you'd better get refund. Unless you feel sorry about it. . . ." The salesman handed over 200 won and the gentleman left the store in light steps as though he had enjoyed his playing. In contrast with their heated argument, the result turned out to be ridiculously flat. But the old man felt satisfied. It was because of his moderation that the quarrelling ended that easily, though he was scowled down for a couple of times. The young man should not be ignorant of this. He would for sure change his mood. This was what the old man expected. Hence there would be a certain change in the young man's attitude in dealing with the old man. At this thought the old man became needlessly excited. What made him still sorry about was the fact that the customer was obstinate till he got the refund for the price of the bird. But the old man thought that didn't matter at all, if he bought a bird in place of the customer. And by thus doing he planned to prove his hospitality to the young man. Instantly, he put into practice what he had thought. Before he finished paying for the bird the old man opened the bird cage, which the customer had just returned, and released the bird proudly.

"This is for you, Mr. Spiteful. Since I bought a bird for you, don't be spiteful any more."

After the bird disappeared out of sight, the old man was paying for the bird commandingly with his afternoon income. But right after this he made another mistake. It might be due to his overly exulted mood. That wasn't a big mistake, for the old man didn't think that would turn out to be a mistake. And even when he recognized his mistake, he couldn't figure out the reason.

"Then, where on earth did you get all these birds?"

The old man's mistake was to utter this one sentence. At this somehow carefree tone the young shopkeeper slowly turned his head toward the old man after quite for a while. The old man's expression suddenly became contracted. The young man was scrutinizing the old man behind the white metal-brimmed spectacles. Even when the old man turned his eyes from the young man, the storekeeper kept on watching the old man. A cold and heavy threat was hidden in his eyesight. He was apparently angry with the old man. The old man at last perceived that he had made a mistake. It was clear that something in his utterance had offended the young man. The old man regretted his rashness.

"Well, it is a matter of fact that you have to get all these birds from somewhere else. I was just curious about the way how you can get these birds. . . though, it might be none of my business to know. . . ." The old man was mumbling as if to make a clumsy excuse for his mistake, while studying the young man's face. The old man thought in truth that he had no necessity to know how to gather the birds. Though it was not quite clear to him whether his inquiry about the birds had offended the young man, the old man thought that it was not wise to make the young man angry with such a meaningless matter. But his excuse came too late. The young man's anger didn't seem to be easily melted away. Without saying a word he kept on sending his gaze upon the old man, who was utterly confused, till the old man became too depressed to try to make any excuse, and till the old man would leave the store not to make the young man vexatious any more. The old man overdid his effort to avert the young man's temper. And also his mind was buoyed up thoughtlessly. He felt like he was spraying ashes on a bowl of rice ready to be served.

5

To make the situation even worse, the old man made another mistake on that night. Something very strange had happened at night in the park forest. The old man made an uncomfortable bed upon a bench in the park. Around two or three o'clock in the morning he heard that someone was stirring around in the park. He was awakened by the sound and raised his head under the overhead field jacket. An electric light like a long stick was scanning the dark forest. Once in a while the light was fixed on one spot among the branches and a shadow of a man was climbing the tree and picked out the sleepy birds as if they were fruits. The birds upon sudden attack by the light were helpless like blind birds. Those birds which tried to fly away lost their bearings and collided with each other. Some were dropping down to the earth after striking the branches, and others were falling down headlong. The shadow of a man was continuously hunting the sleepy birds with the electric light. The hunting for the birds was strangely easy one.

"So like this the birds returned to the store." The old man heaved a sigh of admiration. However, the admiration couldn't last long. Was it because the glow of the electric light was too strong in the quiet darkness? The old man, who was watching the hunting, hidden in the darkness, felt his heart trembling for fear. Without any specific reason, he was afraid of the light and the shadow of the man who was manipulating the light. His body was shrunken as if he were watching something he should not see. Furthermore the light was approaching to him near by near. Though he couldn't tell why, the old man felt that the night hunter should not be notified of his being watched. He became more and more nervous and restless.

The nearer the light approached him, the deeper his head was dwindled into the field jacket. But the light didn't miss him. Finally the light hit upon his head. At the same time his head was hidden completely in his jacket. The light didn't have any intention to leave the old man alone. The light which hit upon the old man was soaking into the jacket. He preferred to close his eyes, but still the light was penetrated onto his eyelids.

At last heavy footsteps were nearing toward him and stopped a few steps away from him. And for a while just a bright light was penetrating him. The old man, breathless in his jacket, was enduring the shower of light. The light removed away from him after it had pressed him down into suffocation. Soon the footsteps were heard slowly dying away. But the old man was like a frog marked by a snake.

The old man wanted to have a glance of the figure of the hunter disappearing into the darkness. But in fact he couldn't dare to stir under the jacket. He was waiting with his eyes closed to hear the footsteps die away.

When he awoke up next morning, the old man wondered whether the last night's event was not a dream. But it wasn't a dream. If it were not a dream, then the old man had made another mistake to vex the young storekeeper. He had a hunch that it would come true. He didn't watch the young man with any intention. Last night the old man acted so cautiously that he didn't give to the young man any clue for his watching. But he couldn't feel secure at all.

The old man hurried his morning business of collecting coins, so he could get to the store about one hour earlier than usual. As he had expected, the storekeeper's face didn't show any sign of his knowledge of last night's event. Since the customers crowded in the store from the morning, the owner might not have time enough to pay any attention to the old man. The young man didn't display any special bearings. That made the old man feel more suspicious and uneasy. The old man thought that he had better appease the young man.

"Among my inmate friends there was an old guy nicknamed eel, and he missed this store much more than I did." The old man started with a topic that could attract the young man's attention.

"That guy was counting days with a hope that someday he would buy a bird at this store. He had continued to write letters and waited for his son's visit to the prison. For that old guy to buy a bird was his biggest wish, more than anyone else. It's your store that provides those helpless guys with the most cherishable dream and hope."

In spite of the old man's flattery, the young storekeeper didn't stir at all. The old man continued his talk patiently regardless of the young man's cool response.

"Someday I have to buy a bird for that old guy. Though he wished to buy a bird, that guy couldn't accomplish his wish. Unfortunately he died in the prison two years ago. I think it's my duty to buy a bird for his spirit. . . . Then I must buy at least ten more birds for those guys in the prison and those who were dead. . . . But it's worth while for me to do that, since I am just fresh from the prison. Sure, I'm willing to do that trouble. . . ."

It should be the most attractive sound to the young storekeeper to express some intention to buy birds. The old man did his best to wrench his brain to appease the young man. Still the young man didn't show any sign of response. His face revealed that he didn't pay any attention to the old man's mutterings.

And even there seemed to be a grave sense of warning hidden under the infrequent glance of the young man. Though he couldn't make sure by his own speculation or feelings whether the young man was contemplating over the last night's affair, the young man's obstinate silence made the old man restless and uncomfortable. The old man despondent was cracking his brain for a while. Then it occurred to him that he had made a grievous mistake.

—That's it. How come didn't I think about it till now. . . . It was reminded to him that he didn't buy a bird this morning. He remembered not only this, but that he had avowed to buy more birds for his friends. Yet he didn't buy a single bird. He was wondering at his absent-mindedness. Then he remembered that he didn't buy a bird, the old man didn't get excited with the idea of buying a bird. He was not in a position to attend his own mood. He was dominated by the young man. Now he had to buy a bird for the young man regardless of his own state of mind. He felt more depressed at this thought. But soon he consoled himself.

—This is also for those guys in the prison, too. When did I buy any bird for the young man? This is all for my friends and for the birds as well.

The old man finally made up his mind and counted the coins in his pocket. Then he poured the coins on the cashbox. Fortunately the number of coins were more than twenty, for he was not in a position to bargain for the price of the bird.

"Well, this one is for that terrible guy whose nickname was 'king's grave caretaker'." According to the turns in his mind, the old man thought for a while of the old guy with a southern dialect who used to pillage the goods at the ancient tombs. Then he freed the bird out of the bird cage with more fervent desire than usual. Still the young storekeeper kept his hands off this business. When the old man handed over the coins, the young man didn't change his expression except his cold eyes, as if he were substituting someone else. The old man didn't feel better after he bought the bird. He didn't have any strength left to stay at the store any longer. He had no business at the store and no intention to utter any words either. At last he left the store with the icy silence of the young man left behind. He felt his footsteps more tired and heavier than before.

6

The old man was haunted by the searchlight during the night at his bed in the park woods. The search beam was straightening like a long stick into the pick-black night and the birds hit by the search beam were fell down from the trees like autumn leaves. And the searchlight was wandering around the night forest in search of the old man. He was irritated and anxious. And he was also dreadful and impatient. Sometimes the search beam was mercilessly thrusting over his field jacket. And sometimes it was searching madly around the forest missing him wildly.

The old man was suffered from a nightmare in which he was repeatedly chased by and then caught by the light until the day broke. Actually the old man didn't see the search beams. He only dreamt about it. When he awoke up in the morning, he felt stunned as if his brain was not his own. He didn't even think of doing his morning routine. Though he could think of his morning business, he wouldn't have enough energy to do that. He sat down disheartened watching the morning woods, as if he were soulless. Until the morning sun was high up in the eastern sky, the old man barely started to move. But he stubbornly refused to pick up the coins that morning and walked down toward the store with unsteady gait.

The store was already opened and customers gathered there were no fewer than other days. But the old man didn't buy a bird this time. Though he couldn't buy a bird, since he didn't pick up the coins, he couldn't feel a sense of loss. He didn't even show any sign of approaching to the young man by studying the pleasure of him. He was just sitting across the store and dejectedly watching the customers busy with buying birds. And he left store when the morning business slowed down with as tired and heavy footsteps as he came to the store. He didn't reappear at the store even till the dusk was hanging over the park woods.

It was in the morning as usual that the old man reappeared at the bird store in exhausted and shabby shape. But he didn't buy a bird... Neither did he try to talk to young storekeeper... As he did the day before, the old man was just watching the bird transaction and left store when the morning business slacked down around the noon. For several days he repeated this routine. He always left the store silent with the same tired and worn-out feature. However, this time the storekeeper showed unexpected gesture.

"Maybe your son, who is supposed to meet you, has been blocked to traffic, or has just turned away from you." When the morning business slacked down for a while, suddenly the young man started to talk to the old man.

"As long as I remember, it has been more than a week since you are freed from the prison. Then how come your son didn't show up yet?"

Was it that much irritating on his nerves that the old man was just lingering around the store without any special business? Or was it that the young proprietor might have suffered in his business due to the fact that the old man no longer bought birds. Anyway the young man changed his strategies and began to ridicule the old man. It was apparently his wicked plan of casting the old man away far from the store.

"Why don't you write him again? Your letter might not reach your son yet. What is your address? I mean your son's address...."

He didn't show a little bit of his hostility for the old man's not buying a bird. He'd rather choose some annoying for the old man to make himself troublesome to the old man, and thus finally to force the old man to leave the store by himself.

"He's waiting for his son. His son has built a palace-like house in his hometown and is coming to get his home." Sometimes the young storekeeper mercilessly gibed at and humiliated the old man to those customers.

"How far does he come? As far as a hill.... You should have a happy dream of your filial son every night."

However, the old man didn't show any sign of taking notice of the jeerings. He just turned his face away as if he had nothing to retort back. When the young man exceeded in his sneering at the old man, he just with a sad glance stared at the young man and sighed a deep sigh quietly as if he pitied the youngster's reckless imprudence. Nevertheless, the old man had no intention of departing from the bird store. He was not that kind of man who was threatened to leave the store by the young man's harassment. He had still something to do.

"For all the guys I have to buy birds. . . . To buy a bird for each of them. . . ." The old man muttered to himself. He thought that he should not forget his friends in the prison. He gave a pledge to himself for several times that he couldn't leave this place without buying birds for those poor guys in the prison. He simply felt reluctant to buy birds. When he bought birds, he couldn't feel cheerful and light-hearted as he did the other days. However, he made an excuse for himself. He thought it was because of the nightmare. He expected that if he would have the dream of that harassing searchlight no longer, he could feel better and enjoy his buying birds. As long as the birds dropped from the trees like autumn leaves at the attack of the searchlight, and unless he could comprehend the reason why the birds couldn't leave the park and were caught again and again, the old man didn't feel like buying birds again. Buying birds would be a silly game like children's playing hide-and-seek.

Then one night, another mysterious thing happened to the old man. He was enduring a cold and uncomfortable sleep on the park bench. Around one o'clock in the morning the electric searchlight was scanning the park forest. It was not a dream. A night hunting with the search beam as its guide had begun. With any groundless fear, his body shrank. But fortunately the situation was entirely different from the other night. The search beam didn't find him out yet. Or probably the night hunter might evade the place where the old man was making his bed. The light didn't seem readily to approach to the old nothing to worry about the light. However, once shaken over sleepiness, he couldn't go back to sleep as if nothing had happened. At last he pulled down his field jacket collar and slowly sat down on the bench. And with calm hand he fumbled in his pocket and took out a cigarette butt and lighted it. It was just at that moment when he was about to light the cigarette butt covering the light with his jacket. Flap-flap. . . . Something from somewhere in the darkness came flying and stuck into his jacket. He was surprised and quickly extinguished the cigarette light. Then he rapidly touched the thing stuck in his breast. Soon he could figure it out. That was a bird driven away from the forest by the searchlight. When he touched something soft and warm, he knew that instantly. The bird taken away outside the jacket seemed to be scared and its heart was throbbing heavily. It was apparent that the bird was flying toward him when he lighted the match.

"This guy driven away by the light was again flying toward the light . . . . How senseless birds are. . . ." The bird's absurd behavior seemed unusual and funny to the old man. However, the old man might misread the situation. He thought for a while about the way how to treat the bird. He couldn't let the bird fly off. The bird was scared stiff. The bird hunted by the light was again frightened at him. It was not possible to let the scared bird fly into the darkness.

He decided to free the bird after making it feel at rest. He carefully put the bird on his palm and gave soft push on its shoulder with his other hand. He waited for its response even withholding his breath. It didn't show any sign of running away from his palm. Whether it knew his intention or not, the bird was staying there with softly throbbing heart.

Then the bird started to peck his palm with its small bill as if it felt secure in his motionless palm. And finally the bird pushed its head out through the two palms and cautiously looked out in the darkness. The old man felt secure. He thought he could let the bird fly off. He took off his hand, pushing the bird, with gentle motion as not to startle it.

Then something strange happened again. The bird didn't show any intention of flying away. It continued to cock its head. He felt more and more strange. His motion became more cautious. There was nothing he could do except watching the bird. He aimlessly watched the bird. With strong perseverance he overcame himself till the bird felt more secure. Suspense and strangeness made him endure the waiting.

The bird came completely to feel secure. It seemed to regard that the old man's hands were leaves of the tree. While pecking the hands and cocking its head to him, the bird seemed to have no intention of leaving his hand. The old man thought that he should do something. He decided to put the bird into a test. He aroused its attention by making a dry cough not too loud to make the bird startled. However, its reaction made him more puzzled. At his coughing sound the bird waved its tail as if it paid some attention to it. Then it descended down on his knee. He was rather amazed.

However, the old man felt like understanding all the stories of what had happened in the past days. The bird was apparently familiar with the old man. He couldn't think otherwise. It was clear that the bird recognized the old man and came to him.

"Well, you guy, now I know. . . . You were the bird which got the wings from me and returned to the park forest. . . ." The old man strapped the bird with his two hands slowly and softly. He muttered to himself as if the bird also could catch the meaning of his word.

"I understand your belief. Thus we become members of the same family while believing each other. I don't know how you think about it, but the young storekeeper of that store down there would be the same. Though such a wild bird like you could have belief, this stupid man didn't understand that simple reason why you couldn't leave this forest. . . ."

It became quiet around when the search beam had descended down the hill. The old man lay down again on the bench and put his two hands, which clasped the bird, carefully on his chest. Then with his eyes closed the old man talked in whispers to the bird which was softly squirming its warm feathers inside his palm.

"You'd better spend tonight with me like this. Though you feel somewhat suffocating. But I won't let you feel cold. You can do whatever you want to do after I fall asleep. . . ."

7

When he awoke up next morning, there remained nothing of the bird. The old man, however, felt light-hearted than any other previous days. The night sleep without any dream seemed very comfortable for him. The boisterous birds' sounds in the forest were heard pleasantly to him. He was listening attentively to the birds' sounds while forgetting the morning chilliness as if to single out the sound of that bird which came to him last night.

Then belatedly he hurried his movement and awoke up vigorously from his bed. He resumed the collection of coins after a long interval and completely recovered his good feeling toward the young man at the bird store.

"If we trace back to the origin, we who live under the same sky are like members of the same family." As usual when the young storekeeper seemed to have some leisure after busy morning transaction, the old man didn't miss this opportunity to express his goodwill and understanding toward the young man.

"Well, since there should be some affection in your dealing with birds, the birds, which fly off with the wings from you, should attach to your feelings. So it should be a matter of fact that while the affection was communicated, even though between a man and birds, they became the same family members. Thus you and the birds are in the same family linked with that affection. . . . ”

The young proprietor, however, didn’t show any sign of responding to the old man, as if he were more suspicious of the changed attitude of the old man. The old man made a bolder approach to the young man.

“I don’t mean anything else. Though it seemed somehow too late depending on how to figure it out, I, this old guy, want to be a member of this park family. Maybe, in truth, I’ve become an actual member of this family. I only wish you, young man, recognize this fact with generosity. What I mean is that I wish you understand my affection or understanding toward you and your birds.” The young storekeeper still didn’t express any response. The old man continued confidently with such a tone as to prove more clearly how he felt about.

“So I decided to buy again the birds from this day on. That’s because to clear my mind’s debts to those fellows in the prison. But that will be good for both of us. It’s good for you because you’re selling birds, and it’s good for me because I’m fulfilling the wishes of those guys in the prison, and also it’s good for the birds since they can get the wings. Furthermore, if we come to understand each other’s genuine feelings, we can be the members of the same family, and that’s good, too. . . .” The old man continued to mutter as if to make the young man feel comfortable.

“But you don’t need to be suspicious about my talking about same family and so on. To be frank with you, I have been suspicious about that whether my son has really forgotten about me or not. I’ve felt depressed to think that my son forgets about me and let me wander around this place for ever. . . .”

“. . . . .”

“However, to think in other ways, it would be rather fortunate for my son not to appear. As I have said before that I have other reason for not leaving this place soon than to wait for my son, that business did not end at all. As you have approximately grasp the meaning now, that business was to buy birds for those guys in the prison. Unless I would buy birds for each of them, I could leave this place, even though I could meet my son. If he could come up to this place, my business would be in trouble. That's why I can say that it's rather fortunate for my son not to appear here yet. That's to say from my own point of view, but from his point of view, it means that he neglects his own business. And his negligence made me feel heartaching. I even felt impatient. . . ."

". . . . ."

"But such an absurd thought of this old guy was effective only till yesterday. I've changed my mind. Though you could hardly understand me, from this morning I can feel secure about everything. I feel like that my son will soon appear to meet me. Though it might be a mere expectation or feeling of this old guy, anyway, I've been living with belief in those wishes. I've had no other ways except having belief in those wishes. That was the wisdom I've learnt from my long experience in the prison. My son will definitely come to meet me, and will bring his daddy back home. . . ."

". . . . ."

"The only thing that I have wished of you is that to be a member of the same family and as such to have a little belief in what I've said. That I've a son and he will come to see his father in the near future. . . ."

The young storekeeper never made any answer. The customers again began to rush into the store. Leaving the old man alone, the young man quickly turned to the store to mind his business.

The old man again started to wait. But anyway he had avowed to buy birds. He couldn't sit and wait the time to pass by. He approached to the bird cages imposingly. He started to select his own bird among the customers. But his motion was not that of those who wanted to buy birds quickly. With cautious and serene expression he was scanning the bird cages one by one. Sometimes he paid a special attention to a bird in the cage as if he were ready to buy it and sometimes to draw the bird's attention he pushed his fingers into the cages. But he kept well his impulse under control. Like this way he was cherishing and enjoying as long as possible his opportunity of buying a bird and letting it fly off, while enduring his impulse. It's rather correct to say that he was persistently waiting till he could search for it, while he was enjoying himself. It could be either the time when he and the storekeeper were left alone in the store after all the customers were gone, or something like a fateful waiting for a bird for which he was going to buy wings. Anyway, he didn't show any sign of buying bird soon. He was likewise waiting for the time to pass by till the crowded customers were gone after finishing their games.

The young proprietor was refilling the empty cages with the birds brought from a secret hiding place inside the store. Though he had no opportunity to look into the hiding place to see how many birds were hidden, it seemed that the young storekeeper had never left the hiding place vacant of birds. Especially the young storekeeper never left the outside bird cages empty during the morning time. It seemed that there were in the hiding place always some surplus birds waiting for their turns to fill up the empty cages. Whenever the young man came out of the hiding place, he always carried the birds as many as he wanted. This day the young man was already filling out more than twenty empty cages. The old man was continuously controlling his impulse in front of the newly-filled bird cages. Then, at that moment, something very strange happened at a certain bird cage. When he stroke the door of the bird cage with his customary gesture, the bird in the cage flew to his finger with fluttering wings and stuck to it. The old man pushed his finger farther into the cage. Then the bird in the cage started cautiously to peck his finger with his small bill once or twice and then without any fear it sat on his finger. Then the bird was looking into his expression with its small eyes while waving its tail. He stood in front of that bird cage with stunned expression as if his feet were rooted in the ground. A yellow smile was spreading over his wretched mouth. And there ended his long-looked-for moment.

"Why, of course I can recognize you now. . . ." After he muttered to himself in a low tone, the old man talked to the young man proudly. "I'll buy this one today." He fumbled into his pocket and counted twenty coins. And without waiting for storekeeper's answer, he started to open the cage door. He pushed his hand through the open door and wrapped the bird cautiously with his palm. Then he raised the bird high up to his nose as if he were handling a precious thing, and murmured to it as if he were talking to a man.

"Now you have to know this. This is not the place for you guys enjoy yourselves. It'll be the last time for me to buy you, so you should fly far away from here till you feel pain in your wings. . . ."

The bird in his palm fluttered its wings a couple of times as if to urge him. Now the old man took a position to let the bird fly off. He pushed the tip of his fingers under the fluttering wings and raised it up high in the sky. It was at the moment when he was about to free the bird murmuring something to himself. He drew the bird again to his breast. Something might be wrong. Then he scrutinized under the wings. It was evident that some scars were made when something like scissors cut off the inner wings. The old man put on a stunned and confused look on his face as if he couldn't figure it out what scars did mean and how that happened. At last a certain strong fire of indignation was aroused in his eyes, after he was quietly looking into the scars. Putting forth his utmost strength in the hand clutching the bird, he looked directly at the young man who was stealthily watching the old man. His eyes burning with fierce indignation made him even look different. His mouth and hands were trembling with fury. The old man, however, was too well tamed to control himself. He was enduring his indignation without uttering a word. The fierce heat was dying away from his eyes burning with anger and hatred. Then already in the place of hatred and indignation a residue of quiet sadness was forming. He turned his eyes away from the young storekeeper and looked at the blue, high autumn sky with longing heart. Though he couldn't behave as usual because of the old man's unusual manner, the young storekeeper behaved naturally as if he were watching some one else's business. The young man could neither interfere with him, nor completely ignore the old man by turning his back to him. And finally when the old man uncovered the scar under the wings, the young storekeeper took an uncomfortable manner like the one whose hideous secret was revealed, but he was receiving the old man's face directly with somewhat brazen and indifferent expression as if not to lose himself. The old man, however, perceived the situation and controlled himself. With this affair the relation with the young man ended. The young storekeeper soon restored his confidence. And he was making mystified smile to the old man who was looking up at the sky. When the old man drew his eyes quietly from the sky and again looked at the young man, the storekeeper was leisurely watching at the old man with strange smile mixed with sneer and pity.

8

The thoroughfare led from the city was stretched white under the autumnal twilight towards the south. The autumn sun lost its fierceness after passing noon time. The old man closed the collar of field jacket and was persistently moving his tired footsteps toward the south. A bird taken from the house where the birds were freed was endlessly moving its bill and claws in the right hand of the old man, which was hidden in his breast to function as a windshield.

"Though you feel uncomfortable, be patient a little more." The old man murmured to the bird as if to talk to his fellow wayfarer. "My feet aches me very much, but we have to find a village while the sun is up. We may have to walk like this for a couple of days. So we can't sleep outside from the first day." The old man continued to walk toward the south. Once in a while he turned his head back to the city as if to find some excuse for hurrying his worn-out steps from the sky of the city which was distancing in his back. Whenever he turned his back to the city, the old man talked proudly to the bird in his breast.

"It was really the best thing we could do that we left the guy at the store. And furthermore the cold winter will soon make rush for the city. Such a small thing like you cannot survive the cold. That guy should have known that, too. Well, you sure have a look at that guy who stood with stunned face and just looked at me without saying a word. Just when I was about to leave the store with you. . . . Oh, of course, I did pay him the money worth while."

A group of persons, who were coming from the opposite mountainside and heading for the city, were passing by the old man, talking loudly. The old man stopped talking for a minute and let the city dwellers come by him. After the noise of their talking died far way from his back, the old man resumed his talking.

"It was very fortunate thing for me to have saved the wages of the last half years term in the prison. It was because of that money that I could bring you out of that place. Actually I decided not to spend that money till I get to home. . . . But I do not regret. Of course, I am not regrettable for my deed. I don't care about the money. . . . With this shabby attire and with an empty hand, I'm wondering how they will think of me, but I haven't been changed at all. . . . No, no, my son is not that kind of guy who would mind of my presence like this." He shook his head forcibly. The bird in his chest moved its claws as if to answer to him. The old man, who stopped to feel the bird's movement, had put a satisfied smile on his face. "Well, it's well done. It's good to leave that place." He started to speak again while resuming his journey. "My son will tell me that I've done well. Unless we left that store, we should have almost spent the winter there." The old man was murmuring with hazy eyes as if he were enjoying somehow more mysterious and precious secrets of his own. "You will come to know soon. It was really well done that we started our journey to the south. The south is much different from the north. The bamboo forest is still green in the winter. The winter will be all right where there is bamboo forest. I'll bring you to the bamboo forest. At the back yard of my son's house there is bamboo forest, too. There are a lot of bamboo forest. . . . Then you fly to that bamboo forest. Then you spend the winter there. . . ."

The old man's face was shined with brightness and happiness, like that of a man who was enraptured in a wonderful dream. He kept on walking and muttering. " It was a pity that such a small thing like you hurt your wings so much. You've to wait for the wings to grow up while resting at the bamboo forest. Till you can fly over the sky at your will when it's getting warm next spring. Of course, if you don't mind, you can winter at my son's home with me, but probably you don't want to do that. . . ."

The evening sunshine was losing its warmth. The white thoroughfare, stretching to the south in meandering ways, was getting gradually hazy from the far way place. However, the old man could feel the warmth of sunshine upon his back. As long as the sunshine was shining upon him, the narrow street stretching to the south was glowing clearly and warmly. The sunshine was more like a light of soul which endlessly shines his innermost heart. Following that warm and happy light tirelessly, the old man was murmuring incessantly to the bird, which once in a while makes movements with its claws in his breast. "But you have to watch out. To find out a village where there is a house, a house fenced with citrus trees, a roof-tiled house with a tall red brick chimney, a house with a wide yard and with bamboo forest at the backside. . . . That is the place in the south where we are heading for. Though it is not that easy to find out as we may think it is. But. . . well, I'm wondering how you can figure out how warm it is in that southern village. . . ."

Chŏm-nye

As the evening deepened more people continued to arrive. Everyone from the village, the upper and lower villages as well, came. The moonless night with only a few stars twinkling here and there gave a somber look to the thick growth of summer squash vines and the corn stalks. Only the field stretched out in front of the house, from the base of the gate, like a sea of water gave a feeling of endless calm. This field was not the property of the people within the gate.

The cramped room, the room with the wooden floor and the yard all together were very small. That was it. Not even three kan,* the kitchen and the wooden floor room taken together were the same size as the small room. There was no place to stand so that some of the young men left as soon as they

* kan : measurement to indicate the size of a room or a house. 1 kan = 36 sq. feet.

came, went outside and sat on their heels on the dike along the rice paddies. The young women made a huge commotion as they pushed against each other in the cramped area. The women carrying babies on their backs yelled and complained that their babies were going to die. However, not one showed any sign of leaving. It was very unpleasant the way in which those shabby and dirty people pushed and shoved each other in that cramped space. The smells were enough to send shooting pains to the head each time a breath was taken.

Chŏm-nye had died the night before. Shortly past noon of the following day her father and Pok, her fiance, had already carried her body out and buried it. Not one of the neighbors had come to help or to watch. But, all of them came together that night, as if by appointment, to watch the special kut* which was to be performed in order to help the dead to make a safe journey to the other world.

They all knew that her death had been unusual. All of them, too, had gone to the blind fortune teller for a protective charm in spite of the fact that her body had already been put into the ground. This was done to prevent Chŏm-nye's ghost from getting control of them. The old superstition that once the spirit of a young bride took hold and did not let go was real to them.

What could have been the reason for so many people gathering together? Although not one of the villagers had come to the house before the burial it would seem natural that someone might have stopped in afterward. But, no one came. However, at the rumor of a kut the whole village came. Not one came for Chŏm-nye's sake or for her family. The rumor of the ghost of the rooster having taken possession of her body, and bringing on her death, spread to all of the nearby villages. In spite of the fact that the night was dark and only a few stars twinkled in that moonless sky the reason for the large crowd was because of the connection between Chŏm-nye's death and

* kut : an exorcist rite performed by a shaman.

the house of Hŏ Seung-ku.

Hŏ Seung-ku was well-known throughout the area for his great wealth. The rumors of his wealth had spread to the capital city of Seoul. Did these poor people come to the kut out of sympathy for Chŏm-nye? Not at all. These poor people who crowded together came out of an intense reverence for the rich man. Their feeling for this man was much the same as their reverence for a God whom they would honor. If her death had been the result of an illness and had no relation to the house of Ho Seung-ku these rumors concerning her death would not have started. If that had been the case perhaps no one besides her family, her fiance and several of the closest neighbors would have come to watch the kut.

The death of a bride or that of a young unmarried woman usually gets more attention than that of a young girl. The peach-like fuzz of girlhood was still visible on her forehead. Her family was afraid of starvation. In order that at least one member of the family could escape the pangs of hunger, and although she was not yet fourteen, Chŏm-nye's marriage was arranged with a man named Pok who worked in the kitchen of the local wine shop. This was the reason that after her death she was referred to as that bride or that young girl.

Why would her family arrange a marriage with a man who worked in the kitchen of a wine shop? It wasn't because of his money or his good character but because the person who became his wife could also work in the kitchen beside him. In a kitchen there was always plenty to eat. For those who feared starvation above all else it was enough to think only of sending a daughter to a place where she would have food to eat.

The only problem was that the marriage couldn't take place immediately after the engagement was arranged. Both of them had to have at least one set of clothes. Even if the groom were to wear what he had the bride had hardly a decent piece of clothing to wear, nothing appropriate for a wedding. There were eight people in her family, an eighty-year old grandmother, her father and mother, and four younger brothers and sisters. They were barely able to manage enough food to keep death from their door, and, of course, could not even think about clothing.

Chŏm-nye's husband-to-be, Pok himself, was in the same boat. He ate at the restaurant and received a monthly salary of 500 wŏn* He couldn't afford to buy material for so much as a rayon chima* and an unlined summer chŏgori.* He couldn't dream of getting married immediately but if he saved his salary for five months he would be able to afford the wedding.

One month, two months, three months, four months, five months passed before Pok had saved 2,500 wŏn. He took the money and went to Chŏm-nye's house. Her mother insisted that he go to Seoul that very day in order to buy the material for the wedding dress. She herself ran off to the blind fortune-teller's house to set the wedding date. The date was set for the twenty-eighth day of the fourth month of the lunar calendar.

Pok left for Seoul. He bought enough rayon material for a pink chima and material for a chŏgori, as well as a box of face powder and a mirror which looked like a plaything. He bought one pair of stockings and a pair of shoes made from the inner tube of a car tire for himself. In this way he used the entire amount of 2,500 wŏn.

Chŏm-nye's grandmother and mother were concerned that he hadn't bought at least one yard of material to make pŏsŏn.* Instead of the mirror and the face powder they reasoned that he should have bought material with which to make pŏsŏn. Pok told them that his cousin who lived over the hill had ten baby chickens and had promised to sell two of them and give the money to him for his wedding. Pok then went to his

* wŏn : unit of Korean money.
* chima : long skirt, a wrap-around with a high waist, worn with the chŏgori as part of the traditional Korean woman's dress.
(See "The Ritual at the well" footnotes.)
* chŏgori : short-waisted top with long sleeves and worn with the chima.
(See "The Ritual at the well" footnotes.)
* pŏsŏn : white cotton-filled foot covering worn with the Korean dress and inside of rubber shoes.

cousin's house and returned with two of the chickens in his arms which he put down in the yard of Chŏm-nye's house.

Although it appeared to have been planned that way it was only by chance that the twenty-eighth day of the fourth month of the lunar calendar was the sixteenth of June on the solar calendar. This was the date set for the wedding of Hŏ Seung-ku's daughter, Sun-haeng.

Chŏm-nye's family, besides all of the tenants too, knew that Sun-haeng's wedding date had been decided during the winter season of this past year. But, what they didn't know was that the date, according to the lunar year, was the twenty-eighth of the fourth month.

Ten days before the date of the wedding, beginning with the relatives, people started arriving from all directions. The tenants came also. This was how Chŏm-nye's family came to know that her wedding date was the same as the young miss, as Hŏ Seung-ku's daughter was called. There is nothing unusual about weddings being set for the same day. However, as for Chŏm-nye's family who had been tenants of the Hŏ family for generation after generation, it was not permissable to have the wedding on the same day. Besides that, they had been unable to tell the people in the big house that Chŏm-nye was even engaged to Pok. They were afraid that the big house wouldn't approve since Chŏm-nye often went there to help the young miss. They were embarrassed to be sending off a child who was not yet fourteen to be a bride. The day for her wedding was only a few days off and yet Chŏm-nye couldn't bring herself to tell the young miss that she was to be married on the same day.

Even if this hadn't been a problem the big house was a terrifying place. It was frightening to go to a place where one always had to be very careful. The children, and the adults as well, from the time they stepped through the gate, felt inhibited and the words would not come. Not only once, but many times they would go to the big house with the intention of saying something, only to return unable to have uttered a word. Although they had done nothing which deserved a scolding they could only hang their heads and remain silent. The words would not come.

No one knew when this had all started. Generation after generation watched and learned; the grandfather, the father, and the son, each learning from the one before.

Chŏm-nye's mother was distraught and once again sought out the blind fortune teller. She told him about the problem with the date and asked him to name another acceptable one. The fortuneteller shook his head and told her that the only other possible date for a wedding, other than the twenty-eighth of the fourth month that would be appropriate, was the fifteenth of July. And, he added that if they were married at any other time both of them would either become blind or crippled. Chŏm-nye's mother was horrified at the possibility of her daughter and her new son-in-law becoming lame or blind. In addition to not being able to have the same wedding date as at the big house, the family had yet another reason for changing the date.

Chŏm-nye was happy for the delay in her wedding. It wasn't because she didn't want to get married, but because the chickens would become large in three months time and two big chickens would bring at least 700 wŏn. She had made up her mind to forget about the padded white poson and instead, with the money for the chickens, she would wear a printed rayon chogori. Since the weather would be warm it really wouldn't matter whether or not she wore pŏsŏn. She wanted to look like Sun-i who as a bride the summer before had worn a printed rayon chŏgori and painted her face with a creamy liquid makeup. The thought flashed through her mind that she would have been happier if Pok had bought liquid makeup instead of the powder.

She didn't know enough to be surprised or envious when she saw in addition to the ornaments, the toilet articles and the bedding of Hŏ Seung-ku's daughter, Sun-haeng, the more than one hundred pair of pŏsŏn which alone filled a three-tiered chest to the top. Chŏm-nye didn't give it a second thought since Sun-haeng was the daughter from the big house.

It might be well to mention that Sun-haeng had more than ten sets of chŏgori, one hundred in all, in her wardrobe. There were five sets of chima, three sets of petticoats, and three sets of pantaloons. There were ten ibuls.* There was a very large brass wash basin, one a trifle smaller, and one an ordinary size, besides a medium size, a slightly smaller one, and three more to make eight in all, the last of which was very small. There were five chamber pots, brass, glass and ceramic ones. Besides this, there was cotton cloth, calico, ramie, brocade, silk, lace and satin, bolt after bolt of all kinds of silks, satins, cotton and linen. No one knew how many wardrobes were filled to overflowing. There were gold and jade hair pins with hanging decorations, a diamond ring, twin gold rings and a gold ring which all together cost more than 300,000 wŏn. A fur stole for winter wear was said to be worth 30,000 wŏn.

If one were to ignore the cost of everything but the value of one necklace at 30,000 wŏn and compare this with Pok's salary of 2,500 wŏn with which he bought the pink rayon material for a chima, the white rayon chŏgori material, the face powder, the mirror, his socks and the shoes made from the tire of a car, Chŏm-nye still would have been unable to comprehend the vast difference between the two houses. She hardly seemed to care nor was she able to understand because of the world of difference between those who have money and those who do not. Even though Chŏm-nye or her family had been aware of the discrepancy it wouldn't have surprised them in the least. Anyone in the same class as her family would have reacted much the same.

It would seem natural that one would question why it was that some lived one way while others lived another way. These people had never cut their finger nails or toe nails because they

* ibul : part of bedding which is used as a blanket and originally made of layers and layers of cotton encased in bright brocades.

had worn down from work. And yet, they never had enough to eat. Did they never question why the others dressed so well, or had enough to eat, or lived without stress and strain? These thoughts never once crossed their minds. It never occurred to them to be resentful nor to feel regret or to think that their treatment was unjust. It was taken for granted that life in the big house was one way and for them another way.

This way of thinking had become second nature, a tradition. These traditions and habits were not the practice of one or two years or something that had been carried on for ten or twenty years. These wretched habits and these tragic traditions were the result of hundreds of years of living like slaves.

It came about that Sun-haeng's huge and magnificant wedding was held on the eighteenth day of the sixth month of the solar calendar or the twenty-eighth day of the fourth month according to the lunar calendar. The bridegroom had no family but as the bride's side was wealthy, and besides she was an only daughter, this wedding was their one opportunity to stage a grand and lavish affair. For this reason the celebration took place in the yard of the bride's home. The huge yard of over 1,000 pyŏng* was filled to overflowing with people standing outside the gate as well. It was impossible to count the hordes of people who came to watch the ceremony, to eat, to look at that luxurious and splendid affair, and to see the bride. Some said there were about ten thousand people while others insisted there were at least ten times that number if there were any at all. More than ten friends of Hŏ's son who worked in the county office came, as well as people from Seoul and some Americans. The house of Hŏ Seung-ku hosted a huge wedding celebration.

Six days after the celebration the bride and groom loaded all of their splendid belongings, jewelry and household goods into a freight truck and accompanied by her mother and brother,

* pyŏng : measurement used in measuring areas of land, size of house.
1 pyŏng = almost 4 sq. feet.

left for Seoul.

It was four days later that one of Chŏm-nye's chickens was caught when it strayed inside the wall of the big house to the vegetable patch.

Hŏ was good at being cold and heartless at other times, too. Was he weary from all of the wedding preparations? Or, had he regretted spending well over one million won on his daughter's wedding? Was he feeling lonely after having sent off his only daughter? Whatever the reason he tied the chicken by its wing to a long pole. He deliberately fastened the pole to a post of the wall with a rope. The chicken appeared to be piercing the sky suspended so high up in the air. Frequently in the past, too, some chickens that had gone inside that fence reappeared with broken legs. Others were stoned to death. However, this was the first time that one had been tied to a stick for punishment.

At the present time, Chŏm-nye's house was the only one with chickens. It was impossible to raise chickens without first building a coop. The fact was that everyone's chickens, without exception, went into Hŏ Seung-ku's yard.The houses encircled the wall of the big house with its wide expanse of yard. The wide fields on the inside with an abundance of food contrasted sharply with the small fields outside of the yard.

"Get rid of all of those chickens," he ordered.

No one disobeyed. Some of them disposed of their chickens immediately whereas others locked them up with the intention of eating them later. When these chickens became sick they, too, were killed and eaten. Some others sold their chickens and some even sent chickens as presents to the big house.

Chŏm-nye's house was the only one left in the whole village with chickens. The chickens were not allowed to run loose. One of the chickens got out when she was putting in a bowl of water. She was worried that this one would go through the fence into the big yard. She stood guard. However, when she left for a minute to gather greens to put in the supper pot that evening the chicken slipped through the fence.

The clouds were snowy white. Was it the blue of the June sky and the vivid green of the trees which made the clouds appear whiter than usual? The white fleecy clouds rolled together into one big mass and then began to unfold as they spread across the sky. Chŏm-nye's chicken hanging on the pole looked like one of the white clouds. The screeching of the chicken penetrated the white clouds and floated away across the sky.

"Who does this chicken belong to? So you thought you could raise chickens as you wished. Just you wait and see, all of you. You think the world has changed and you don't know who the boss is. You didn't think about that, now did you? Even when you're shaking in your boots you think you can stick your nose up in the air, you good-for-nothings. You think the world has changed so quickly and you're the bosses now? You bastards. Why, you, you, you just think you can stand before me with your hands behind your back. That's bad manners. You good-for-nothings! You don't know a thing. You don't even know how to be thankful. All of you? Who do you think is responsible for where you are today? From your grandfather's day and before, all of you bastards. You there, in Tae-chŏn's house. From your grandfather on down don't you owe everything to us? And, now look, just because you think you can let your chickens run all over the place why we don't have anything to eat in our house for a year," Hŏ Seung-ku commanded as he stood in the center of his empty yard.

Chŏm-nye's father's name was Tae-chŏn. Evidently Hŏ Seung-ku had heard that the chicken belonged to her family. Chŏm-nye and her family had already heard that their chicken had been tied on a pole and was hanging up there in the air but not one of them could go before Hŏ Seung-ku and confess that the chicken belonged to them.

After liberation with the adoption of the tenant law the house of Hŏ Seung-ku sold most of their land. The land not directly attached was sold off piece by piece, in one and two thousand pyŏng lots and five and six hundred pyŏng lots. The remaining land was either in several thousand pyŏng amounts or ten thousand pyŏng sections. No one wanted to buy that much land. The whole lot was put up for sale but there was no one, as there might have been previously, who wanted to buy that large of a piece of land. Now Hŏ was in a big hurry to sell this land to the tenant farmers.

Imagine a farm of ten thousand pyŏng with one hundred tenants who under the old system experienced more days with an empty stomach than with a full one. Where would they get money to buy the land? The land each has cultivated will be sold. When the land is sold the tenant can no longer cultivate the land but must move. From that day on starvation begins. Chŏm-nye's family was one of these.

The landlords were sure that with the enforcement of the land reform law the tenants, due to their large numbers, would become cocky and loathsome. On the contrary, there was no way of knowing how much grief this mass of ignorant and illiterate farmers endured.

Some of the farmers, fearful of losing the land, sold their homes and their household goods as well as their ox and the pigs and the chickens before they were ready for market. When that was not sufficient they took out a loan with a high rate of interest in order to hold the land.

There were others who after having borrowed the money from the loan shark, purchased the land and then gave the deed to the loan shark for safe keeping. A previously unheard of situation developed whereby the moneylender accepted half of the crop realized from the land in lieu of interest on the loan. Many of these moneylenders were landowners who felt safer, in these uncertain times and not knowing what the future held, having the deed to their land in another's name and taking half of the harvest. The price of grain was high and they realized a greater profit than if they had collected interest.

However, not everyone was able to purchase land in this manner. Moreover, in this small farming village, there were no moneylenders who was able to lend that amount of money. In addition, the land areas were large and there was no way the tenants could borrow the necessary amount. Chŏm-nye's family tilled only a two hundred pyŏng portion of that ten thousand pyŏng piece of land that stretched before these houses like a sea of water. The land had been up for sale for quite some time and because there was no buyer Hŏ Seung-ku had ordered the tenants who cultivated the land to buy their portion.

It was always a frightening experience to be confronted by him. Could anyone have the courage to go to him in this present situation? Chŏm-nye's family could do nothing but caution her not to cry so loudly for fear of being heard by Hŏ Seung-ku. The tenants were uneasy and the landlord had become unusually irritable. In former times even though there was no reason for the landlord to fly into a rage, when he did, he would say something about taking away their land if they didn't shape up. All of the landlords confronted their tenants in the same manner and tone of voice. Due to the land reform act they were afraid that the tenants would not show them proper respect but would act in a haughty and disgusting manner and this they could not tolerate.

It was natural that the landlord became more sensitive and that his nerves were set on edge. This made the tenant more uneasy and put him in a continual state of panic.

Chŏm-nye's family, unquestionably because of this relationship, was unable to tell the big house about her engagement and also the change in the wedding date. On the other hand, the reason why he was so cruel to the chicken could have been due to the fact that his nerves were on edge from weariness over hosting his daughter's wedding. However, this wasn't the reason. Nor was it because he regretted having spent over one million won on the wedding. Nor was it due to a feeling of loss upon the sudden departure of his only daughter and the loneliness that took hold of him. When he went back into the house his heart felt light as if a heavy load had been lifted. He was pleased with himself and felt a great sense of satisfaction although the wedding had cost him more than the huge sum of one million wŏn. He would have had the same feeling of satisfaction if he had spent twice as much.

"One never knows how long one will have his fortune," he said over and over to himself.

He frequently asked his son, "What is the world coming to? Will we go communist or will we go democratic?"

His son would answer that they would just have to wait and see how the provisional government would work out in order to know.

Then Hŏ Seung-ku would say, "I don't suppose that with the establishment of a new government we will return to the past, would we?"

He asked this question in the hope that by some chance the good life they had known in the past could somehow return. The reason that his nerves were on edge was for no other reason than this.

This tenant farm system which came into effect upon liberation was a blow to the landowners. The only reason for their abnormal nervousness was due to anxiety over their own insecure future. The tenants were forced to undergo a great many visible and not so visible sacrifices due to this anxiety. If Chŏm-nye's chicken was one of these sacrifices, then Chŏm-nye's death, too, was the result of the sacrifice of the chicken.

However, her death could not be blamed on the spirit of the dead chicken having taken possession of her body. She died because she was hit by a stone thrown by Hŏ Seung-ku when she took her white chicken down from the pole up in the air.

It is natural to feel anger if someone has died as a result of being hit by a stone and to call the person who threw the stone a vicious scoundrel. But, Chŏm-nye didn't die on the spot. The stone was not very big and it left only a scratch on her forehead. It drilled such a small hole that it looked as if a finger had been pressed on her forehead.

The moon was shining bright as day on the fourth night

since her chicken, looking like a white cloud, had been tied to that pole. That white, cloud-like chicken was all the more visible in the light of the moon. The chicken's cry was more pathetic on that moonlit night and so it was that Chŏm-nye unnoticed came out of her house, quietly pushed open the side gate to the big house which hadn't been closed, and went into the yard. She took down the pole that was bound fast to the post on the wall, untied the chicken, and holding it to her breast she stepped carelessly on the lettuce, the spinach and the tomatoes in the garden. As she was hurriedly going out of the side gate she felt like she had been hit in the head. At the same moment she heard someone yell something about a rascal. She felt dizzy but since she had no idea what had happened she kept on running. When she arrived home she fainted on the spot after putting down the chicken which she had been holding. Her family guessed that she had climbed through the fence, taken down the chicken and that the blood on her forehead was the result of her having crawled through the fence.

Her mother made a lump of soybean paste and pressed it on her forehead. The flies had laid eggs on the paste and it was swarming with maggots. In the event that a wound bled from being injured on a farm implement these county people either rubbed on soybean paste or put on ashes, or applied shrimp paste alive with maggots, or rubbed kerosene on the bleeding part. More often than not they became well with no other complications.

Chŏm-nye did not get better, but died. She became delirious after the application of the soybean paste and her face became swollen. Later on the swelling spread to her entire body and the following day she died during the night. The only thing she talked about in her delirium was the chicken. Chŏm-nye's chicken breathed it's last several hours before she died. Her mother was touched by the way in which her daughter had taken such care of her chicken that she threw some rice, which was more precious than gold to them, to the chicken. But, the chicken, its eyes closed, only panted and would not eat. Then with its last ounce of strength, it gave one final cry, stiffened its legs and went limp.

As Chŏm-nye's delirium increased she said, "Mother, the chicken is nothing but skin and bones. See the chicken is wearing such a beautiful summer chogori." Then, she added, "The chicken is dancing so fast even though it doesn't want to get married. My goodness, how is it, oh my, oh my, the chicken, the chicken. . . . The chicken is so beautiful with that creamy makeup. My how beautiful. . ."

In her delirious state she opened her eyes wide and reached with her arms for the chicken as if to take it down from the pole to which it was tied up there in the air. This was the reason that her death was said to be caused by the spirit of the chicken.

The room was cramped. There was no place to stand because of the narrowness of the wooden floor room and the yard. Some of the young men came and left while others sat side by side on the dikes along the rice paddies. The young women crowded together into the small wooden floor room and in the yard created quite a commotion as they twisted and brushed up against each other. This mangy looking crowd of people packed into that small space was most unpleasant and with each breath the smell gave one a splitting headache.

In the small room her mother, looking like a rotted tree which had fallen over, her father, grandmother, grandfather, four younger brothers and sisters, and her fiance, Pok, all sat with vacant stares on their faces. The mudang's* face was clearly visible although the oil lamp flickered. The place where Chŏm-nye had laid was spread with a layer of white rice. A pine tree branch stood in one corner. A long, white piece of paper hung in tatters from a branch. The piece of paper on the branch was to be the medium through which

* mudang : a shaman.

the dead Chŏm-nye would communicate with the living, her parents, her fiance and her brothers and sisters.

The mudang, carrying a gourd of water into which ashes had been mixed, sprinkled the corners and the ceiling of the small room and the wooden floor room. Then, taking clear water, she went over everything again in the same manner.

The mudang yelled to all of the spirits to leave, those in the street, those in the room and to the spirit of the chicken that had taken hold of Chŏm-nye. Although the narrow wooden floor room and the small room had corners, walls and ceiling there was no space to move so the mudang just splashed the ash water and the clean water from where she was standing. Whether it was because of the dimness of the wooden floor room, on top of everything else, the ash water and the clean water splashed on the family members together in that small room made them look all the more like dead wood. In that light, too, the people standing looking on appeared more shabby. The mudang scraped on a basket while her young nephew took a hold of the branch.

"Look here. Mom, Dad, Grandfather, Grandmother, Pok, my brothers and sisters, I'm going. I'm on my way to heaven."

It is easier to arouse people to tears at night so that as the mudang's voice trembled some of the people echoed her and started to cry.

"Oh, Mother, what a shame. This sweet sixteen year old hasn't been held once in the arms of her future husband. Oh, what to do?"

From that time on the mudang began telling lies. Chŏm-nye's husband-to-be, Pok, hung his head. The wedding date had been set and then she had died. But, as for being sweet sixteen, Chŏm-nye was still only a young girl of fourteen. In reality she didn't have the slightest notion of what marriage was all about. All she knew was that she would no longer be living with her mother, brothers and sisters but in the market place where she would work together with Pok in the wine shop. She hated leaving her family and living apart from them. But, she would be able to eat her fill at that wine shop in the market. She had liked the part about Pok's trip to Seoul when he brought back the pink rayon material for her wedding clothes and the doll mirror, as well as the idea that with the powder she could look like Sun-i when she was married last year with her face powdered white.

"Oh, Mother, what shall I do? How could that chicken dare go to the big house when I had worked so hard taking care of it? Why couldn't it have been satisfied here? Why oh why, did it go through the fence to the big house?"

"Then I felt so sorry for you that I took you down and your ghost took a hold of me. You should be torn limb from limb, you rascal chicken you! You're good for nothing else but to be put into a stew. . . ."

It was apparent that the mudang had also heard the rumors that the chicken's ghost had taken possession of Chŏm-nye.

"Because it happened at the big house they'll only be more mean. You ate a year's worth of grain so you should be strung up for three months. That's cheap, you know. If they had tied you up for a year that would have been only what you deserved. You should be made into soup."

The mudang, as well, appeared to stand in awe of the rich man.

"Mother, all of you, go out and get rid of that one rascal that's left."

The mudang's nephew, who was clutching the tree branch, suddenly jumped to his feet and trembled all over as he stepped outside. Those out in the yard who had been shoving and pushing again started to move about.

The young man held the branch in his hand as he went around the yard looking for the chicken.

Chŏm-nye's mother followed behind him chanting, "Don't worry, Chŏm-nye, we'll get rid of it, the chicken. . . ."

Her voice was choked as if the tears had run down into her

throat. The mudang continued to rattle on and on that the chicken had to go. Both Chŏm-nye's father and her grandfather stared stupidly like two old fools and her grandmother muttered in a muffled voice which she wiped her tears on the corner of her chima. Pok sat quietly while her brothers and sisters looked from one face to another with their mouths hanging open.

"Mother, get rid of everything, all of my clothes. What use is it to keep them? Just take care of my dear brothers and sisters and throw my things away. Get rid of all of them."

Again the nephew got up abruptly and started to shake. He shook harder than when Chŏm-nye had talked about the chicken and the stick started to rap and even jumped. As he held the branch in his hand he turned around and looked all over the room for the clothes. The tattered piece of paper hanging on the branch fluttered. The oil lamp flickered all the more and nearly went out.

Once again Chŏm-nye's mother got up and said, "Child, child, don't worry, we'll throw it away, get rid of it, you don't have to think about the clothes you bought. You just go safely along the road to nirvana." Since she was crying and talking at the same time it was not at all clear what she had said.

As before, the branch shook violently. Chŏm-nye's mother took down from the shelf an old, frayed box which was smaller than a sewing basket and opened it. The branch turned the contents upside down and took out the pink rayon chima and the white unlined rayon chogori. Those nicely folded clothes were a mess and in the flickering light of the lamp the rayon chima had the lusterous look of an expensive material. This was all there was of the clothes and things that Chŏm-nye had gotten ready to wear.

The mudang, however, was sure that there were more clothes and other things that a bride-to-be would be getting ready for her trousseau and she continued. "Mother, get rid of it all. What good is it to keep any of it? Get rid of it." She ordered in a loud voice, more insistent than before.

Her mother lifted up her twitching face and said, "Child, there isn't anything left. It's all put out." She rubbed her hands together and chanted as if she were part of a chorus.

The mudang realized that in fact this was all there was and said, "Mother, Father, Grandmother, Grandfather, goodbye. Take care of yourselves. You, too, my brothers and sisters, and you, too, Pok stay well. We're still like one even if you didn't hold me in your arms even once. I'm going. I'm on the road to nirvana."

The gasping and the hard breathing grew less and less as the mudang brought the kut to a close. She knew that nothing else would happen no matter how long she sat there scraping on the basket.

Without anyone being aware of it Chŏm-nye's mother made her way out through the room and into the yard. She took the last chicken from the chicken house and put it down in front of the mudang. Next, instead of taking the beautiful wedding clothes which the shaking branch had pulled out, she took the clothes which should have been on the corpse, folded them and placed them in front of the mudang. Pok had kept saying up until they left the house for the burial that the body should be clothed but her mother had insisted that if they intended to call the mudang in to perform a kut it was necessary to have her chima, chogori, pantaloons and slip. There was no way out. Although her mother was sick at heart at the thought of burying the naked corpse the body was not clothed.

This kut had to be performed by the end of the second day after the death. Besides that, it was believed that unless the kut was carried out a great disaster would result. In addition, the marriage hadn't taken place and the family was frightened to death because the death of a bride-to-be was not normal.

After the mudang had been given the clothing and the chicken she stood and stared for sometime at the rice that had been scattered on the place where the body had lain. The family stared, too. The mudang ran her finger through the rice announcing that Chŏm-nye had become a flower upon her death. The outline of a flower appeared on the rice which was spread out on the floor. The mudang swept up the rice with the imprint of the flower and put it into a small bag. She didn't actually do it herself but her nephew held open the bag while Chŏm-nye's mother swept up the rice and put it into the bag. The mudang and her nephew left, taking everything with them.

As soon as they were gone, in no time at all, the others left. No one was left in the wooden floor room nor in the yard. Only Chŏm-nye's family and Pok sat in silence in the small room. Their shadows moved ever so slightly as the oil lamp flickered in the breeze. They were like stone statues. The children were as quiet as the adults except the youngest who was the quietest of all because he was sleepy.

Upon leaving the house all of the spectators groped their way along the dark road. Not one of them said that Chŏm-nye's death had been a tragedy. They talked about their fear of the ghost of the chicken and about being afraid of the spirit of the bride. They were still excited over the splendid wedding of Hŏ Seung-ku's daughter Sun-haeng.

There were eight brass wash basins, more than ten sets of chŏgori, five sets of ten each of slips, and how many ibuls of silk brocade? Were there four or five ornamental hair pins? Each one shared with enthusiasm what was known, what had been seen, or what was only rumor. No one said anything about how Pok had saved 2,500 wŏn for five months in order to buy the chima and the chogori. No one mentioned having heard that Chŏm-nye was raising the chickens in order to sell them and, then forgetting about the poson material, make a chogori just like Sun-i wore when she was married the year before.

The Ritual at the Well

It was the day of the annual ceremony for the cleaning of the well. The head of the village had been rushing around since early morning telling everyone to come to the well for the ceremony. I quickly put away the breakfast things and went out to the well.

The ceremony went like this. First, the well was cleaned out entirely so that the water ran clear. Then water was ladled into a brass bowl which was placed on a small table. It was believed that a prayer asking for a plentiful supply of water said before this table would be answered. In addition, all of those who drank the water would receive the five blessings of long life, wealth, health and peace, respect and many sons.

In the villages where this ceremony was observed every house, without exception and whether or not it had a well, considered the attendance at the ceremony to be a personal obligation. I participated but not because I had some special wish like the others. We had our own well and a year might pass without my having used one drop from the village well. I took part because this was a community affair in which all joined in together.

By the time I arrived a considerable number of villagers had already gathered together under the large shade tree and were busily binding together two tin kerosene cans which were then tied to a thick straw rope the size of a swing rope. This was the bucket which would be used to draw the water up from the well.

The well was situated right in the center of the village next to the rice paddies and the fields. This marked the boundary line of the road that passed in front of the village. No one knew when or by whose hand this well had been dug. It never ran dry although this village of around forty households drank the water year in and year out, season after season.

> Forty families. What then is significant about the amount of water that a village this size might drink? Not only forty families, but forty families with forty different kinds of daily chores. The amount of water used by only one of these families every day is no small matter. Of course, well water flows continually, but this is not my concern. Nevertheless, if water wasn't that plentiful how would one house manage with forty different daily uses for water? Let's not take one year or even one month, but only ten days and calculate the amount of water that is needed. How many earthenware pots must be filled? It would be quite a number. Wouldn't a large pot have to be filled at least ten times?

There was always enough water even though these forty households, with the exception of two or three in the whole village, never missed a day of going to the well.

> I am not only speaking of one year, or once or twice a year, but about the beginning of this village down to the present and on

> into the future when the descendants will multiply and increase. The offspring of these villagers multiply without ceasing like the endless gushing forth of the well water. The continual use of this water could be symbolic of an eternal year. The word eternity is devoid of any particular meaning when it is written without any special thought. But if one closes the eyes gently eternity becomes a heavy, endless word, weighing on the conscience.

Although like the others I felt an obligation to take part in the ceremony, more than that, I believed in honoring the flowing of the water from eternity to eternity. By contrast, I found the villagers' observance of the special ceremonies to the rocks, the earth and the trees repulsive. The well ceremony was different.

A large tree stood a short distance from the well. The tree was so large that three men could encircle it with their arms. Large branches spread out from this huge trunk. These many branches had fostered more than their original number of boughs so that the tree was unusually broad and tall. I didn't know the name of the tree and like the villagers, I, too, called it the big shade tree. Its spreading branches tangled together nearly shut out the sky along with the great quantity of leaves that grew out of those numerous branches. It didn't seem oppressive for the sky to be covered like that since the lovely shade tree was a more beautiful sight to see than the sky.

No one talked about whether the seed had been planted by hand or had quite naturally fell and sprouted by itself. The tree had never been fertilized or pruned and yet it had grown into a magnificant shade tree with only the help of the wind, the sun and the rain.

The ugly looking bark of the trunk was like a rock. It not only looked like a rock but it felt like one. An ax or a saw could not make a dent in it. The abundance of leaves on the tree, compared to the other trees, was noteworthy.

Before anyone was aware of the coming of spring, and when

the fierce winter wind was still dragging its tail across the sky, a wind blew in from a far corner of the earth. It was more like a fragrance than a breeze, like pollen from a flower it blew so gently. That shade tree appeared to be the first to feel that stirring within which heralded the coming of spring.

The limbs which spread out from that stone-like body were the very first of all the trees to be covered with delicate green buds. This tree was the first to give shade. The local villagers were not the only ones to use it as a resting place. Other villagers, who happened to be returning from their fields at sundown by way of the shade tree, would fill a bucket of water to the brim, drink it with the water dripping down the sides, and then sit down and rest under the tree.

Some had oxen on ropes while others had only a hoe in their hands. Those with an ox would first tie the nose ring to a stone at some distance from the tree.

There was a constant stream of young boys and girls washing barley or rinsing vegetables or carrying water. It might well have been that those from other villages came not only to rest in the shade but because it afforded a good look at the young girls and boys who came to the well.

The tree had other reasons for its existence. During the summer time the merchant who sold household wares and the one who repaired the cooking pots set up shop under this tree and carried on their work here. Not only was the tree used in this way to make a living but on the Tano* Festival in the spring a swing was tied to the tangled boughs and the young girls, their bosoms swelling like cotton candy, swung back and forth feeling free and light.

The children could easily climb up into the branches where they sat and pretended to be riding a horse. They looked down on the houses of their friends and called for them to come out and play. Some of the children swore at the children they nor-

* Tano : a special festival held on the fifth day of the fifth lunar month or in May or June of the Roman calendar.

mally disliked while others caught cicadas. There were even some rascals who urinated from the branches. Others called out to the girls they especially liked.

As the older boys circled around underneath watching the girls coming and going at the well they couldn't recall when it was that they had stopped climbing the tree.

With the coming of spring the young men went to the far off mountains to gather wood. On their return trip they would pick an armful of cloud-like azaleas to throw down at the feet of the girl of their choice under this tree. It was here that the mulberries from the mulberry tree were divided and eaten, making the lips look as if they had been dyed a deep wine red. Others sang any song which happened to come to mind in their attempt to squelch the passion that was swelling inside.

The rice paddies and the fields spread out down in front of the well and the shade tree. At the place where the paddies and the fields ended a narrow river flowed along holding the blue sky in its bosom. There were mountains to the back, mountains to the east and mountains to the west. A portion of the south was also closed off by mountains. It was overwhelming; there were so many.

Besides this smaller river there was also a larger one. This dreamy, idyllic village on the sand was surrounded by these two branches of the Han River which flowed on as far as the eye could see. It was nature at its best, the sky, the flowers and the shade trees. To all who came here, this village gave the impression of having an intimate relationship with nature.

The man who repaired the cooking pots and the merchant who sold household utensils talked about how peaceful and blessed this village was. If this had been true then there could be no hunger, illness or ragged clothes, only love and singing.

"Come on now, let's get going," ordered Mr. Yun with the pockmarked face as he struck the gong again and again.

He lowered the tin cans down into the well. The striking of the gong set the rhythm of the pace. Mr. Yun's job was to sound the signal while Hak-su and Wŏn-pae were assigned the job of dumping the buckets. The young girls held the end of the rope and the young men grabbed the front.

One strike of the gong by Mr. Yun was the signal to drop the tin cans into the well. Two strikes of the gong was the signal for filling the buckets and pulling them up. At three strikes Hak-su and Wŏn-pae were to empty the buckets.

At the signal to lower the buckets into the well those who were holding to the rope had only to walk forward. When the signal for filling the buckets and pulling them up was given the young people had only to walk backwards. Everyone had to stop in their tracks at the signal for Hak-su and Wŏn-pae to dump the buckets. That was all there was to it, the same thing over and over. It was that simple. There would have been a sufficient number if only one person from each of the forty households had been ordered to participate. It was not strenuous to move backward and forward and then to stop.

Everyone was in a happy mood as it was more like play than work. Some softly sang snatches of songs. The deaf man from Chang-wŏn, a vacant stare on his face, kept muttering meaningless words over and over. Sometimes he stumbled on the stone-like roots of the tree as he was looking around. He was watching Mong-bun, Yŏn-sun, Suk, Hong-sun, Kap and the other young girls behind him. Hong-sik, Pong-su, Ggo-maeng, Tŏk-gyun, Sŏk-yun, Pok-gil and the other young men, too, glanced behind.

There was a good number of young men and women for the size of the village. However, if I were to reveal the reason why at this time it wouldn't be appreciated.

It was apparent that Yŏn-sun and Tong-bun, along with the other girls, didn't mind the backward glances of the young men. Although the girls chattered on and on, when the eyes met they hid their faces which had become as red as fire.

"Hey, you rascals, you. Careful! Your eyes are going to be stuck there in the back of your heads," teased the pockmark-faced Mr. Yun.

Although the deaf man didn't know the reason for the

laughter he, too, joined in.
faced Mr. Y..n. Although the deaf man didn't know the reasoı
for the laughter he, too, joined in.

"You too, deaf guy. Get hold of yourself. Say, Hong-sik and you other guys, take hold of the rope. Do you want to let go of it? Watch it!"

Everyone was laughing and in the excitement Yun started to sing a song.

"Uncle Pockmark, you're getting excited again," said Pok-gil.

"Excited, who's excited? I'm just mad from having been doused, that's all. I really feel great." He raised his shoulders and started to move his hips in a dance.

Sure enough, at a closer look, Mr. Yun's clothes were soaking wet. It was all because the bucket got tipped the wrong way now and then when the deaf man and the young men didn't follow the beat of the gong.

"You rascals, you. The only reason you can take part is because you're pure, that's why. Who said you could come out here and scout for bride material? Whoopee, I feel so good I could fly. Whoopee!"

He began to sing a familiar tune. It made little difference that his voice wasn't particularly good. They all began to feel good because of him. He abandoned the beat and raising the gong high in the air started to pound it repeatedly.

"So, you guys, sure enough, you can only take part because you're clean and then you go and sneak side glances at the young gals."

There is a phrase in the mudang's* chant which refers to this being clean. And, the fact that they were clean was what made them feel good.

This is the important part of the story which I want to explain. The women who were either pregnant, or menstruating, or who had slept with husbands the previous night were unable to participate. However, the men were ex-

* mudang : a Shaman.

empt. Men or women who had been in a home where there had been a death, or who were in mourning clothes in observance of the death of parents, or widows who were in mourning for husbands were not allowed to take part in the ceremony. The reason being that they were considered to be unclean. It was believed that a terrible misfortune might occur if any of these people were to participate.

Naturally, there would be a large number of young women missing and with the exception of a few adults all who remained would be the children. If the little ones who weren't really strong enough were excluded, the young men and girls would be the only ones left. Why were there so many? I am still not ready to tell you why there were so many unmarried bachelors and single girls in such a small village.

The sky was full and the breeze announced the coming of fall. The cicadas cried from the shade tree. Whenever a gentle breeze blew over the fields and the rice paddies down below the well and the shade tree, the green shoots along with the soybeans, the sorghum, the red beans and the cotton plants mingled together swelling like the waves on the sea.

> How can it be said that these are one and the same when the sea is a dark blue and the plants are a dark green in color? That is a legitimate question. However, I am not talking about color but of the feeling that comes over one while walking back and forth holding only to the rope. It is that aimless feeling, that wanderlust stirring which takes hold of the heart, that helpless feeling when looking at the sea.

"You rascals, get gone, you . . . ha, ha, ha!"

They were all taken by surprise at the shrieks of Yun who looked like a drowned rat. He had been drenched with the water from the overflowing bucket.

"Yah, just look at that. God, but now you won't feel the heat. Great isn't it, Uncle?" One of the boys teased the drenched man as they all again broke out in laughter.

"Well, so what if I got doused with water. If you get a good laugh out of it, well, so what? Whoopee! For heaven's sake, let's whoop it up. Whoopee!"

The wornout hempcloth knee breeches clung fast to his seat as he moved it back and forth. He began to sing again as he continued beating the gong. He was a sight. The young people were of an age that they laughed to see horse droppings so it was quite natural that they all burst into laughter. There was nothing to do but stop temporarily. Yun seemed to have forgotten his assigned task, too.

"Look here, Chang-gun, stop your laughing. We'll be back where we started. Come on now."

The village head put a damper on Uncle Yun's comedy routine. It was apparent that Yun respected the village head and without further delay he stopped shaking his hips and began to sound the gong.

Hordes of dragon flies were flying around. The cicadas cried loudly. It was about noontime as the sun was high in the sky. The tree gave shade as usual but still the shirts stuck to the sweaty backs.

"What happened to the makkŏlli* they went to get?" asked the grandfather from Koryŏng who was feeling rather hungry standing there behind the others.

"If it were anything like last year we would at least be getting barley rice to eat . . ." retorted Chil-gun as he swallowed with loud gulping noises.

"Well, you ate well the year of liberation didn't you? What was it now, rice cakes, meat, wine . . . . "

"That wasn't because of the well, that was just a party."

"Anyway we ate like that!"

"Isn't anyone going to treat . . . ."

Even if they had eaten a huge breakfast of meat, rice and many side dishes, it was noontime and they were famished. All it took was for one person to mention food and immediately

* makkŏlli : fermented liquor made from barley or rice.

the talk was of nothing but food. Loud swallowing sounds were heard from the front to the back.

As recently as last year Landlord Ch'oe had given rice mixed with barley. And, the year before, the year of liberation and using the well ritual as an excuse, rice and money had been collected from each house so that all ate well on wine, meat, rice cakes and a large assortment of vegetables.

But, this year was different. The people in this village had formerly lived by cultivating and harvesting the land of one man, Mr. Ch'oe. I had no idea when this had all begun because it was that way when we moved here. I guessed that they had been living like that for a long time.

With the coming of liberation, Landlord Ch'oe hurriedly moved his family to Seoul. He left his house and land in the hands of his steward, a Mr. Lee, to dispose of them. When the villagers learned what he had done they were crushed and wondered how he could have possibly done this to them. Everyone in the entire village burst into tears just as if some terrible calamity had happened to them. After some time they went to the man who had been entrusted with the care of the property and talked the matter over.

The steward was upset and said, "I'm with you, I understand."

He rubbed his chin as he sympathized with them. Their difficult lives and the gaunt faces he saw daily pained him.

The steward went to the landlord in Seoul and reported on the plight of the villagers.

The landlord responded by saying, "I told each one of them to buy the land which they had worked and they didn't. So, what am I supposed to do?"

He refused to listen.

The steward asked, "Is there any way they could have gotten money together to buy the land?"

The landlord answered, "Well, then, there is nothing that can be done about it, now, is there?"

The steward had nothing more to say. The only thing he got

out of the trip was a firm order to sell the land as quickly as possible.

The steward was met with loud cries of anguish and the clapping of hands when he started to sell this land which the villagers had worked. The clamor which they made neither rose up to the heavens nor fell back to the earth. It only turned in on those who had made the sounds.

The majority of Landlord Ch'oe's property was sold to farmers from other villages who already owned their own land. About thirty percent of the land remained in the hands of these villagers. At that, no house had more than two or three rice paddies. Previously they had worked this land which belonged to the landlord and each year had returned his quota of rice. What remained was far from enough for one year, six months or even two months. In fact, it wasn't sufficient for even one month so where would they find the money with which to buy the land? Would money fall from the sky because of liberation?

As a result the lives of those villagers, who no longer had the right to work the land, became a living hell. Those that were able to buy two or three rice paddies could barely make a living but the remaining seventy percent were penniless. They could either do day labor or fell trees and sell the wood. Was piece work available all year? What kind of day labor was possible in a poor village as small as this one?

Many of the villagers went to other places to work during the spring planting, the summer weeding or the fall harvesting. They returned with their earnings. Some went as far away as Manchuria and China. However much they earned it was not enough for even three short months.

Twelve months and earnings barely enough for three months; how could they manage in the long period that remained? There was nothing to do but to go out to the mountains, cut down trees and sell the wood. The pine, the elm and other large trees could be felled with a saw but the smaller ones had to be cut with a sickle. The wood was first cut into firewood and chips and then sold. Not only for one day, or a month, but for twelve months of the year this work continued. They all lived like this, not only one family but the whole village, to the very last person.

The mountains became bare. The forest ranger from the county office feared that the hills would be stripped and his eyes fairly blazed with anger as he chased off the villagers. Although someone in a higher position than this forest ranger had chased them off they had no alternative but to continue because their very lives depended on cutting down trees. They knew they would be imprisoned if they were caught. Hadn't Kap-bok been in prison three months before he was released? And, Pok-gil had suffered for twenty days in police custody. They were well aware of the consequences but what was there to do in such a desperate situation?

> In order to keep the trees on the mountain from being cut down those who are doing the cutting must be told to stop. In order to get them to stop a world must be created in which it is not necessary to cut trees in order to keep from starving.

After Mr. Ch'oe sold his land and moved to Seoul there were numerous rumors about his activities. Some said he was supporting a politician, others that he was setting up an office and some others that he was now the manager of a factory.

Sŏk-yun put the three casks of makkŏlli, which he had brought from the brewery, down under the shade tree. Everyone turned their heads in that direction. The swallowing noises which were clearly audible sounded like the gulping down of water.

"Uncle Pockmark, let's eat," said Hak-sun and Wŏn-pae as they clasped the bucket to their chests and stood dead still.

"That won't do, not at all. If we quit now all we've done has just gone down the drain. Isn't the water still coming out though we keep on drawing it up? This year with such a long rainy season we'll just have to work harder and longer."

"So, what's the use? There is still water even though we keep dumping it. When will we have it all cleaned out so as we can eat?"

"I can't wait any longer," said Wŏn-pae as he threw down the bucket and came forward.

As soon as he did this, Hak-su, also, stepped aside.

"Who'll take their places?" Everyone pretended not to hear Uncle Yun's request. "Hong-sik and Pok-gil, come on, both of you."

"I can't, let's eat and then finish," one of them answered, and then the other said, "I can't either." They both shook their heads.

"Well, but even if you're hungry the proper way to do it is to clean the well first and then to eat. Is this your first time. . . You rascals, you."

An old man nearby swallowed hard and in a fairly dignified tone of voice reproached them as he chimed in with Uncle Yun, "That's right, what do you mean by eating before the ceremony is finished?"

"They're hungry, so just let them have a little something to eat," said the widow who had moved from Seoul in the spring.

Upon hearing the hunger complaints she had gone into her house and came out carrying a huge round wooden bowl filled with bread which had been made from American flour and steamed until soft. This was her first time to participate so that she didn't know that the ceremony was supposed to be finished before lunch was eaten. She wanted to ease their hunger pains.

Her words, "Come and get it," were the only signal needed. They thronged together, the little ones included, like a bolt out of the blue. It was like a swarm of flies the way each one ran, pounced on the wooden bowl and took a piece of bread.

The old man who had cautioned them about the propriety of eating also took a piece of bread. It was an easy matter to insist that it was not allowed before the ceremony was finished. But, once the bread appeared there was no room for stubbornness. All that mattered was who got the bread first. The old man wanted to eat, too. Uncle Yun had a piece of bread as did the deaf man with the sunken eyes who was eating also. Hong-sik and the other young lads were eating, too. It wouldn't have made a particle of difference if the bread had been dirty they would have eaten it anyway.

> Do we eat to live or do we live to eat? This subject is the topic of frequent debates. When I was in elementary school I took part in a debate on the side "People eat to live." It seemed as if everyone present was on the side of "People live to eat." Because this argument seemed more reasonable to me by the time I got up to speak I said that "People live to eat" was more accurate. Our side lost because of this hastily made stupid statement of mine. The students on my side sent disapproving glances my way and reprimanded me. The teachers laughed.

The people in this village neither lives to eat nor did they eat to live. The fact was that life itself was the enemy. Since they could do nothing but go on living they ate because there was life.

When someone died the only comment made by those who watched the funeral procession was, "Now you won't have to starve, that's good."

Do you think I am telling an untruth? No, truly to these people starvation was a curse. They ate but since there was never enough they were always hungry.

The roots of plants and greens were their daily staples. When the spring winds melted the snow on the mountains and the fields, and the green sprouts started to appear, aunts, mothers, grandmothers, daughters, young brides and young girls went to dig up the roots. They carried a basket in their hands and tied a pojagi* around their waists. Every day they went out like this until the harvest in the fall. After the grain

* pojagi : a square piece of cloth used for carrying bundles or packages.

was harvested the period of time for which they had something to eat depended on the rice crop yield. And, the length of time was extremely short.

Until winter set in and reached its peak and the distant mountains were all covered with a blanket of white snow they went out to strip the bark from the trees. The bark of the trees, the dried greens, the germ from the grain of rice and the draff left after brewing the rice wine helped them through the winter.

The winter, more than either spring or summer, was a virtual hell for them. The reason being that all nature died in the winter.

Can you imagine how much they awaited the coming of spring? Winter was a living hell, a time when due to hunger it was impossible to know whether one were dead or alive.

"Spring, spring. Hurry up; spring, come." This was the prayer of the children and adults alike, obsessed with only this one thought.

> "The ones who wait for spring" sounds like the theme of a poem or a novel except that in a poem or a novel those who await spring live in expectation of the spring breezes which give goose pimples. Or the undulating dark blue waves of mist that hover in the valleys and then rise. Or the singing of various kinds of birds or the many colors of the blooming flowers. These are not the same people as those who wait for only one thing, the grass. Green grass, that was it. Only that which could be used as food.

The young men who were sitting around that wooden bowl, more than eleven pairs of swimming eyes, and eating that mushy bread lived by the mountain greens which their young women, or daughters, or mothers, or aunts or grandmothers had gathered and brought home.

Take a look at the evidence. You would know if you saw their bowel movements. This will do for now but it was a real problem for them, to move their bowels. In contrast to someone like myself who has been ill night and day with that problem there are a great number of people in this world who have an enema, or drink warm water or take medicine for constipation. In this one corner of the world, however, there were those who had continual diarrhea because of a daily diet of only cooked greens. And, it was always green.

The day was beautiful. The sky was an unusual azure-blue and the shade was exceptionally deep. The bowel movements, too, would be unusually green in color.

Pok-sŏn's father, his face yellow from hookworm, was there. Hong-su who had been slapped on the cheek by the woman in the house next door when he stole the dregs left from the brewing of the rice wine was present. Pok-gil, from whom two measures of barley had been stolen and who in order to find the culprit had gouged out the eyes of a frog, was there as well. Hung-ryŏl, too, who had eaten soup made from salted zucchini leaves for breakfast that morning was among them also. All were moving their mouths, slurping and smacking their lips in anticipation. Yellow colored eyes, eyes glancing sideways, black eyes, sleepy eyes, sullen eyes, all as big as the eyes of the ox, were staring intently at that wooden bowl filled with bread.

It was like watching a play on a stage. What a shame to watch that scene alone by myself. I wanted to show that very scene to Mr. Ch'oe, their former landlord, who had gone to Seoul and was now reported to be financially backing some important political figure. Not only to him, but to those whom he was supporting. The very ones who, with the help of the rich, rode around in nice cars, lived in big houses, ate well, dressed in style and for whom living was easy. These were the very important people to whom I wanted to show this scene.

> Is this how you see it? Have you ever seen people who lose their heads like this over the sight of white bread? How is it that people who can grow rice should be hungry? What is the reason

why they can't eat their fill of rice? It would be no problem if they could eat barley or some other grain instead of something like rye which is slimy and causes diarrhea.

A few of them were able to wear the traditional Korean dress but most of them looked like beggars. Some wore the uniforms which had been left over upon liberation, patching them over and over, putting patch upon patch. Others wore the judo practice uniforms, winter or summer, night or day, and no one knew the source of these uniforms. Others wore chŏgori,* some were the unlined summer kind and with worn-out sleeves. Those young people who had dressed as extravagantly as was possible before, now, like all the rest, wore hemp or cotton clothes with patched backs and sleeves. Some had never been able to afford to buy cloth and were stripped to the waist. Not one of them knew the cost of silk stockings or the price of enough material for a brocade chima.*

It took a little over forty minutes by train to go the distance of 40 ri to Seoul from this village. How could such a short distance seem so far? Not one of them knew of the machines that were available for making silk and cotton thread by just sitting down in front of the machine and which in a short space of time could produce cloth. They spun their thread on the spinning wheel as had been the practice for years and years. It took all day at the loom in order to weave three yards of fabric for a piece of clothing. At night they worked under the oil lamp. The materialistic civilization of the city was far removed from them. Because they were farmers they had but a few hours of rest in a twenty-four hour day. What was wrong with farming? It was only that they were farmers and weren't able to enjoy leisure time or to have enough to eat but were starving and poorly clothed.

* chŏgori : a short blouse worn as part of the traditional Korean dress.
* chima : the skirt of the traditional Korean dress.

> Don't you agree with me that the world would be a more pleasant place if ten people ate exactly the same amount rather than one person eating well and ten going hungry? Wouldn't the world also be a happier place if ten people were not either too hot or too cold rather than only one person being neither too hot nor too cold?

"As long as we're at it, let's live it up, even if it's only makkŏlli," Mr. Yun said, smacking his lips after finishing the bread, and then going up to the cask of rice wine.

"Yes, good idea." Everyone agreed. No manners or formality was necessary as far as eating was concerned. The elderly became quiet also and seemed to be of the same mind.

"Oh my goodness, the bread . . . we didn't give any to the gals . . ." Mr. Yun suddenly remembered the young girls who were sitting together in a group.

Those faces, with mouths' watering, gathered in front of the wine cask turned in the girls' direction.

"That will never do, now . . . ." But, they didn't seem to be particularly concerned.

"Come on now, this time let's give them first," one of the older ones ordered in a loud voice to the younger ones. This time they were generous as the bread was all gone.

Hak-su filled a bowl to the brim with makkŏlli from the cask and quickly gave it to me. He also brought sour pickles. In the confusion of the moment I gulped it down as soon as he gave the bowl to me. I put some of the pickles in my mouth. They were unusually sour.

My limbs felt tired after drinking one bowl of the makkŏlli, perhaps because it was before lunch. My body was weary and a feeling akin to anger started to fill my breast. In fact it started from the time the bowl appeared. When I saw all of them in front of the bread I sensed the tragedy of their lives. But, strange as it may seem, as soon as I had a drink of the makkŏlli my feelings for them underwent a complete change. I found them disgusting. I wanted to pick a quarrel with them.

Try to understand what I was feeling. You know that it was not because I didn't get any of the bread, don't you?

"Hak-su, come here a minute. Do you suppose you could give me just one more bowl of makkŏlli?" I yelled loudly in the direction of the cask of makkŏlli.

Pong-bun, Yŏn-sun and the other girls along with Hong-sik and the young men, their faces red, laughed at me with mouths wide open. They must have thought it odd for a woman to continue drinking like that.

Whether or not their laughter had anything to do with it doesn't really matter but I took the overflowing bowl from Hak-su, and as before, I gulped it down in one breath. I munched on the sour pickles also but this time I was unaware of the sourness.

My legs were shaking like a leaf. The reason that I was shaking and weak in the knees was due to nothing else but to the way I was feeling. I did nothing but stood there quietly watching those chattering red-faced people. I didn't look at the sky or the rice fields that resembled the sea. Neither did I hear the crying of the cicadas. I just stared at them. It was like watching a play. I was tense. As I steadily looked at them I saw that their eyes had become sleepy, sullen and dull, unlike the wide-eyed look when the bread had appeared. Their faces had become relaxed. In front of the bowl of bread their faces were tight but now the wrinkles on those faces were like gently rolling waves.

"Hey, you over there, is that all you ever do day and night is to beg?" I said muttering to myself in my hometown dialect.

Whenever I was happy or excited this happened. No one had any idea what I had said nor would they have understood if they had known. They kept on laughing and making a lot of noise. Hong-sik and the young men were sending ardent glances in the direction of Mong-bun and the others.

"Now look at this, Hong-sik. Didn't you get a piece of bread and give it to Mong-bun?"

No matter how drunk I may have been I was aware that I

should not have said that. Wide-eyed, Hong-sik looked all around and the others, red-faced and chattering, stood dead still and stared at me as I yelled. The reason that I singled out Mong-bun was because for some time I had liked her name and thought it sweet and cute like the blooming four o'clock flower. She hung her head and her eyes became red.

It was obvious that I shouldn't have said what I did. But, what could I do about it now? I was bewildered and all I could do was to say in a composed voice, "Come now, let's clean out the well."

They promptly got up and dusted off the seats of their pants. It was apparent from the look on their faces that they would like to have taken the time to smoke a cigarette made from zucchini leaves or one of the stale rationed ones. And, yet, they found it easy to get up. They were anxious about getting on with the ceremony and this is what forced them to get up quickly and clean the well. They were uneasy because of their eating and drinking before finishing the ceremony.

I felt as if I had been granted a reprieve. I wasn't worried about Hong-sik or the others. But, what about Mong-bun? How long would her face stay red and would she hang her head?

Mr. Yun raised the gong and sounded the signal. Hong-sik and Pok-gil, the replacements, took the bucket and dumped it. They were lined up as before with the young men in the front and the young girls in the rear. As if to make up for having eaten before the ceremony was finished they appeared to have enough energy to scoop all of the water from the well in one second. I didn't try to take hold of the rope.

How do we judge the abominable plight of these people who sincerely perform the ritual of cleaning the well, then filling a brass bowl full of water place it on the table? I said earlier that although I found the ceremonies performed to the stones, the trees and the earth repulsive I didn't feel that way about the ceremony to the unceasing flowing water.

However, after two bowls of makkŏlli I was beginning to

wonder what it was that made their lives so difficult. Why were they always hungry although they prayed for blessings day and night? At that precise moment I felt such an indescribable dislike for them.

The cicadas crying above my head were as noisy as a bunch of yelling cats. I liked the sound of the cicadas so how could it be that their crying should resemble the sound of a bunch of detestable cats? What if they cried? It didn't do one bit of good. What did it matter if the shade was pleasant and the sky was blue? And, if the fields and the rice paddies down in front were like the sea. It was all nonsense without meaning.

What did it mean to them that nature was good? What if the merchant who sold household goods and the kettle-repair man said that this was a peaceful place filled with blessings?

If the merchants hadn't already said this about the village who among you wouldn't want to write a poem about this scene, or paint a picture? This scene at the well, the two kerosene cans for buckets tied to the thick rope, much like the swing rope, and filled with water then drawn up; or the sight of the young girls standing in the back with the young men up in the front holding to the rope and pulling up the bucket at the ringing of the gong; and the stopping in their tracks; or Mong-bun and the others in the rear in their patched dresses looking like blooming peony flowers though they were starving, and up in the front, Hong-sik and Pok-gil with the other young men.

The beautiful sky spread out above and the cicadas sang from the large shade tree. The fields and the rice paddies down in the front gave the feeling of the sea. Where this ended the small river held the sky its bosom, looking blue as it flowed. The very best of creation was here enjoying an intimate relationship together.

What use was it to say that this village was blessed and peaceful? In this peaceful village with its many blessings there were crying, disease and fighting because of the poverty. Like the clever snake each one waited for a chance to cheat the other.

I said earlier that I would tell you later the reason why there were so many young unmarried men and women in this small village. That time has come to tell you.

Poverty is the reason for the great number of young bachelors and unmarried girls in such a small village. The reason why I didn't tell you earlier was because I wanted to portray this lovely scene of the young people coming out for the cleaning of the well in this dream-like village. The scene at the bowl of bread, and on top of that the two bowls of makkŏlli, made me change my mind. I must confess that I feel differently now than I did before. Right before my very eyes this beautiful picture took on an ugly look.

The reason that the young people couldn't marry was their poverty. Shall I show you how their poverty prevented them from becoming brides or grooms? If you don't believe me come to our village. When you come I will bring out the young men and girls and show you.

From time immemorial weddings have been thought of as an extravagant affair so that those with money planned an ostentatious celebration. Whenever a wedding was planned the first things to be thought of were the glittering clothes and the lavish feast. However, for these young people a very simple ceremony was not in the realm of possibility. It would be reasonable to marry off daughters because the number in the family would be reduced, but in the case of sons, where food was already scarce, there was fear of adding one more to the household. This was the reason for the large number of unmarried young people in this small village.

This wasn't living, this was living only because one didn't die. What good were the beauties of nature? What if the village was like a poem or a picture? A piece of bread was a poem or a picture, that was art.

Look at this. Here I was standing under the shade tree in that tipsy state, right in front of the bucket line. Suddenly the young men turned around and saw a partially eaten piece of bread that had fallen to the ground. The young ones, already having seen it, swarmed around. Hak-su saw one of them pick up the bread and as the child took to his heels Hak-su, in a flash,pulled him back by the scruff of the neck and took the bread away from him. From the back to the front, all eyes focused on that scene.

Slowly, little by little, Ggo-maeng began to tease saying, "Hak-su, you rascal, who were you going to give that bread to, the piece you hid? Come on, tell us. If you don't I'll spill the beans."

"Well, if you've got something to tell, go right ahead. Why I took it to give to my mother, so what?" It was only an excuse. Hak-su's face was flushed and it wasn't due to the wine.

"Hak-su, Hak-su. He's a model son." Hong-sik called out as he turned his head completedly around forgetting his job of dumping the bucket.

"Yah, a devoted son,if that's all it takes, why I'll do it to," chimed in Sŏk-yun.

"That guy told me something. It was when we went to cut wood on the high mountain and he said he couldn't carry his mother on his back but he could carry someone up that steep mountain one hundred or more times. Who do you suppose he was talking about?" As Ggo-maeng said this everyone of the young men, one by one, looked back at the girls.

"You there, Ggo-maeng, even if you don't say it we all know." This time it was Pok-gil who joined in the conversation.

"Can't you keep your mouth shut?" Hong-sik said as he screwed up his mouth and shook his head.

"Come on now, someone's face is already fiery red." Tŏk-gyun indicated those in back with his chin.

They all grinned broadly and turned to look behind. This time Mong-bun's face was redder than earlier under the shade tree when after drinking two bowls of makkolli I had abruptly pointed her out and Hong-sik and the others had teased her. Sure enough, Tŏk-gyun was right. Among all of the girls,

Mong-bun's face was the only one turning red.

Whether or not he knew what was going on, the deaf man looked in turn from Hak-su to Mong-bun. His face was screwed up and he moaned and groaned as if he were carrying a heavy load.

"So, Uncle Yun, you think that Hak-su did that for his parents? You don't really know so how can you say that?" Ggo-maeng interrupted.

"You good-for-nothing, Ggo-maeng, why do you keep on like that? I'm going to wring your neck."

"What are you going to wring my neck for? Why get mad at me just because you couldn't feed your girl friend?" Ggo-maeng, unwilling to give up, continued.

"You young ones, these days you don't have any respect for your elders. . . carrying on like that in front of us." The old man in an authoritative tone of voice seized his chance to speak.

"Yah, here you're not much more than ten and already you're starting to chase the girls. . ." Pok-sŏn's father chimed in.

"What about the twenty years old? Are they just going to stay quiet when those barely over ten start going after the girls?" Uncle Yun said as he came to the aid of the young men when the elders picked on them.

"Come now, let's quiet down. Look at you, here you're over forty and yet you're just like those young guys." The old man who lived in the mud hut said as he clicked his tongue in disapproval.

Yun answered in the same tone of voice as that of the old man, "Yes, so you think you've reached the age when you know all there is to know, so what? Is that what it means to be an adult? To act with great authority, like you know everything, in front of the other adults?"

The old people pursed their lips and glared at Mr. Yun as he joined in the argument.

"Come on, let's stop this talk and clean out the well. It's all because of a rascal like Hak-su that this all started in the first place," Ggo-maeng again goaded Hak-su.

"What's that guy saying that it's all my fault? Let's kill him and throw him out." Hak-su detested Ggo-maeng who like the quarrelling adults also wanted to pin the blame on him. His face flushed with anger.

"Well, if you hadn't hidden the bread in the first place there wouldn't be any fuss now would there?" Ggo-maeng was angry also.

"Hey, what business is it of yours that I hid the bread? I didn't eat it and hid it, so what's the big deal?"

"You guys, why are you fighting anyway on this kind of a special day?" the old man from Koryŏng his veins standing out on his neck said as he came forward, unable to stand it any longer.

Ggo-maeng said, "Sure, you hid it to give to Mong-bun."

The mention of her name only made matters worse.

"You son-of-a-bitch, what business is it of yours. . ."

"Stop it! Look what's happened. Now the teasing has turned into a fight," said Uncle Yun. But, neither of the young men showed any signs of quitting.

Hak-su's mother, hearing the quarrel, appeared on the scene like a whirlwind with a rag in her hand which was dripping with water that was blacker than rat droppings.

"That son-of-a-bitch! It would've been better if he hadn't ever been born. . ." She swung the rag at her son.

The bucket came to a standstill and the quarrelling stopped. All were wide-eyed with their eyes glued on Hak-su and his mother.

The rag, blacker than ink, was wet with old urine and not with water as I had thought. The smell from it made my eyes smart.

The deaf man, a great look of contentment on his face, seemed in good spirits as he patted Hak-su's mother on the back and muttered, "Aba, aba."

Standing there in front of his mother, Hak-su screwed up his mouth as he brushed off his hair and his clothes. His mother looked at him with daggers in her eyes.

"This good-for-nothing son. Why in the hell was he ever born? That's about all you ever do, night and day. So you can't carry your mother up the big mountain and yet you can carry a young gal up one hundred times. Is that right? Well, then, let's see you do it ten times that! She's turned your head. You said you'd hid the bread to give to your mother? What a liar. So then why yesterday did you hide a sweet potato in your load of wood and take it to her house if you are so concerned about me? You're no son of mine. And, of all people, who that slut? The daughter of our worst enemy, why to that wench?"

In her anger she struck Hak-su over and over with her fists. It couldn't have been more embarrassing for Mong-bun. Her face changed from red to purple as she stood there helpless with the rope in her hands.

"Mong-bun, why don't you rest a bit? Just go to your house and rest awhile." I couldn't help but identify with her difficult situation.

In the meantime the anger that had welled up within me seemed to have vanished and my trembling legs and my shaking fists, too, were now back to normal. The anger which I had felt against the landlord dissipated as I was sympathizing with Mong-bun. Without a word, Mong-bun, as if being granted a reprieve, withdrew.

"The world is falling apart, it's going to pieces . . . the children don't respect their parents, what's this world coming to anyway?" the old man from Koryŏng sided with Hak-su's mother.

His words only made Hak-su's mother more excited and she said, "Let me see, what's left at our house? Some touch-me-nots and four o'clocks which his sisters worked so hard to plant and then didn't he take and give them to that slut."

This was directed at Mong-bun who was no longer there. The reason why she became so angry and talked like this was probably due to no other reason than that there was nothing else to do.

"Look at that bitch's yard! It's covered with four o'clocks and touch-me-nots," she screamed at the top of her voice.

The old people, the young men and the young girls stopped and turned in the direction of Mong-bun's yard which was visible from under the shade tree.

At that precise moment Mong-bun's mother appeared. She had either been told by Mong-bun when she came into the house or she had heard the loud yelling of Hak-su's mother who was standing a short distance from the well. In any case, she came out and went and stood in front of Hak-su's mother. As she was about to open her mouth Hak-su's mother, without any forewarning, took the pin from the bun in Mong-bun's mother's hair and grabbed her hair. Mong-bun's mother was firmly caught in her grip. At this point the deaf mute, with lightening speed, took hold of Hak-su's mother and as he lifted her up to move her aside she fell down.

From the time that Hak-su's mother swung the urine soaked rag at her son the deaf man was on her side. However, when the mothers came to blows it was apparent that he sided with Mong-bun. Not only he, but the look on the faces of all the young men indicated whose side they were on. Hak-su, too, felt the same. There may have been no other reason than that she was Mong-bun's mother but it may have been because his mother was the first one to attack.

Although she fell down because of the deaf man Hak-su's mother got up and started in again. It was a frightening spectacle.

"Look at this mess. Something dreadful is going to happen in this village . . . come on, let's dip out the water, the water . . ." the old man, a worried look on his face, said hastily as he saw how engrossed they were in the fight.

"When the hen cries misfortune strikes the house, so when women fight like this something terrible will happen in our village. . ." old man Sun-bo said in a loud voice.

The quarrel between the two started over whether or not

the flowers had been taken, and whether or not the sweet potato had been eaten.

When that was over Hak-su's mother said, "You slut, God will punish you. The land that I worked and ate off, that two majigi* of land, why when it went over to that bitch didn't I cry my eyes out!"

The sweet potato and the flowers were forgotten and the fight centered on the land.

"For goodness sakes! Who told you to sell it? When you said you weren't going to buy it the landlord was selling it elsewhere. So then didn't we sell our iron pot, our soy sauce and kimchi* pots and even the pig which we had fattened. We sold everything and bought the land. If you felt that way why didn't you sell everything and hold on to it no matter what? Why get after me?"

"Ajumŏni,* let's just forget it. My mother's wrong, If you hadn't bought the land why he would've just sold it to someone outside the village, so . . ." said Hak-su, taking his chance to talk.

Hak-su's mother started to pound on her son. "This rascal, this is the way he treats his mother and father in front of that slut. And, if we go hungry, as long as it's for her, that's just fine! All of that land out there to be sold, so why in the world did you have to take the land that we had worked? Oh, that slut . . . I'm really disappointed in that rascal . . . they took our land and still you take their side? You son-of-a-bitch, why did I ever have you . . . that dirty woman. So what? You sold your iron pot, kimchi pots, soy sauce pots, and your pig, too, all of that and bought the land that someone else couldn't? So what? Is that what you have to do in order to feel good? You just wait, I'll raise a pig, sell the piggies and I'll buy the very land that

* majigi : a unit for measuring land area in which 1 majigi equals 5 acres.
* kimchi : a food made from cabbage, or other vegetables, with red pepper, garlic, scallions, ginger and fish, allowed to ripen and eaten as a daily staple with rice and other foods.
* ajumŏni : a title of address for women, literally means aunt.

your family has slaved over. Now I'll just buy all of your five majigi of land. You wait and see, oh my, oh my!"

After scolding Hak-su, Mong-bun and Mong-bun's mother, one after the other, she waited and clapped her hands in the direction of the heavens.

"Mother, why don't you stop and go into the house? Why be bitter against them? All they did was to get together a little money and buy the land we had worked. They didn't do it so we'd go hungry. Why the land we had farmed was just a small piece. We didn't have the money so we couldn't hold on to it. What use is it to say such nasty things? Please go in . . ."

Although the son tried to persuade his mother she didn't listen but only continued in her lament and the hand clapping.

Why did the clapping sound echo from the ground like the beating of the sticks of the night watchman? Was it because the sky was wide and expansive? Now once again I felt different, like when I sensed Mong-bun's embarrassment. My heart skipped a beat and beat faster.

All of them, as one together, those that held the rope, the ones that dumped the bucket, and Mr. Yun who beat the gong, had serious looks on their faces from the time the dispute over the land started. There was no talk of favoring one or the other, or of blame, nor fear expressed over the main cause of this unfortunate affair. Nothing but a drooping of the shoulders and a slowing of the step; that was all.

I was unable to feel hatred for Hak-su's mother who was much more spirited, ruthless and mean compared to Mong-bun's mother. I only wanted to take Mong-bun's mother along with those with the drooping shoulders into my arms. While holding them together like this I wanted to tell them the thoughts that were mounting, seething and surging within me.

> There is no good reason for the two mothers to fight. Although Hak-su's mother insists that they are starving because of Mong-bun's family it is not so. The one responsible for your starving is another. It is Landlord Ch'oe. For decades you worked like

slaves on the land from which you got your food. Although the coming of liberation made your situation better the landlords found things difficult. They felt threatened by their former servants and sold the very land upon which you had slaved so long and hard. Then they went to Seoul where they backed the men in politics. In other words, it is this very same Landlord Ch'oe who put all of his money together to back those who want to start a new government. Right now these very people are using the money which you earned by your sweat and blood in anyway they wish, foolishly and recklessly. How do they use it? These big, rich landowners like Mr. Ch'oe use the money for themselves; backing those who will set up a new government that will take good care of them. Everything is being turned upside down. These kind of people . . . these very people, no different than greedy Mr. Ch'oe, think only of themselves. It doesn't matter what happens to you; if you plead with your hands, or shake your fists, or if you starve, or if your young people can't marry because you are too poor. They have no idea whatsoever how to care for others. They have no blood or tears. These are the very people who are given the task of setting up a government for our country supported with this kind of money. These are the very ones who must rule in order to insure the return of the good old days. The mothers of Hak-su and Mong-bun have absolutely nothing to fight about. Even if they were to tear Landlord Ch'oe to pieces it would be no less than he deserved. Landlord Ch'oe is the one who is responsible for your starving. He is the very one who is responsible for your hand clapping, your first clenching, and for your children not being able to marry. He is one of those with money and land who makes you starve. This is the kind of a world that looks after the people with money and land . . . .

As I was making up this speech in my mind the rope continued to go back and forth. Before I had a chance to say anything a small child yelled, "Look a pig!"

"Oh, my goodness sakes, if it didn't go and get out again..." Hak-su's mother stopped her hand clapping and fighting and hurriedly picked up a stick.

"Here piggy, here piggy."

Hak-su let go of the rope and started to chase after the pig. The pig, having been hit soundly on the rear by Hak-su's mother's stick, ran like a streak of lightening in the direction of the well. As it circled the small table the brass bowl was overturned. When Mong-bun's mother saw this, she went into her house without saying a word.

"Say, that pig is only four months old and already she's looking for a mate. She's been acting like that since yesterday. Here piggy, piggy. . ."

No sooner had these words fallen from her lips than the old people echoed together in chorus, "See here. This isn't right. . . why from this morning on things haven't been just right. . . didn't we tell you that eating before the ceremony was finished wasn't right? It wasn't only the eating, after all there were a lot of things that were said, and the fighting got out of hand, and then that pig comes in heat like that why something bad is bound to happen. . ." They had serious looks on their faces.

These old people knew what they were talking about. Year after year they had observed the ceremony at the well. Those who were considered unclean and therefore not allowed to participate, the pregnant women, women who were menstruating, those who had slept with husbands the previous night, the ones who had attended a family funeral or were in mourning for their parents, or widows in mourning for their husbands. These old people, whose hair had turned white, knew the rules only too well and they had every right to be worried.

The pig circled the well several times and ran around the trunk of the shade tree. Hak-su and his mother ran around the tree with the pig like children who were playing a game of tag.

"Say there, go and chase her over to that side. Piggy, piggy."

"What good will it do to just chase her? We'd better catch her once and for all. What if she escapes around the well?"

"You're right, let's catch her . . . well, we might as well

mate her while we're at it. They say that the pig at the wine shop is a good one."

"Look at them. Stop that dirty talk and strike the gong and let's get on, right now, my goodness what's this coming to. . ."

"Yes, hit the gong. What do you know, a four month old pig already has a yearn for sex, why that's faster than a person. . ."

The old man from Koryŏng had a miserable look on his face after being contradicted in this way by Uncle Yun. But that didn't stop Yun from saying what he did. No objections were raised nor did anyone laugh. Hak-su and his mother were left alone to chase after the pig while the young men in the front and the young girls in the back moved forward and backward to the ringing of the gong.

The cicadas were still singing from the shade tree and the full blue sky looked down on the sea-like fields and rice paddies. Down at the far end the river flowed, more blue than the sky.

"Look at that pig, why is she running in there! She's gone crazy. . . piggy, piggy, piggy."

Hak-su's pig ran into Mong-bun's yard. Her mother picked up a stone and hit the pig hard. She was getting her revenge.

Seeing this, Hak-su's mother again became angry and said, "That bitch isn't afraid of God so that's why she can do that. You keep on like that and I'll tip your house over. Heaven has sent that dumb pig to punish you," she swore and angrily shook the stick with which she had been chasing the pig in the face of Mong-bun's mother.

Mong-bun's mother picked up another stone, and chased after the pig, calling, "Piggy, piggy." She grabbed Hak-su's mother by the throat.

In the confusion of the moment Hak-su's mother threw away the stick and gripping Mong-bun's mother by the throat beat her with her fists and butted her with her head.

Mong-bun's mother cried out, "Look here! This bitch is out for blood." At the same time blood was gushing from her nose.

The young men and the young girls behind them, simultaneously as if to the beat of the gong, put down the rope and ran into the yard of Mong-bun's house. The deaf man ran also.

"Hey, bring some cold water to douse them." Yun ordered Hong-sik to bring the overflowing bucket.

Hong-sik took the bucket, the rope dragging behind, and ran to the house.

"What in the world is this, that ends up in blood?" The old man from Koryong looked as if he were about to cry as he followed the rope.

"Bring some cotton, some cotton. . ." yelled Hak-su as he tried to separate the two who were at each others' throats.

Yon-sun was on her way into the house when Mong-bun appeared with cotton in her hand. Her face was pale.

"Hey you guys, hurry over here, come now, how in the world are we ever going to get the well cleaned?" At the shrill voice of the old man from the wine shop they gathered around as if they had completedly forgotten and suddenly remembered.

By this time the pig had gone into the field of buckwheat and was making a big mess.

Mong-bun was angry. As she lead her mother into the house she turned around several times and sent dark glances in the direction of Hak-su's mother.

Hak-su's mother glanced at the blood on her hands and her sleeve and once again picked up the stick and yelled in a shriller voice than before, "You dirty bitch. You've made our life miserable. Now what more do you want? If I were to take out your liver, eat it and spit it out I still would be mad. Rascal. . . piggy, piggy, you rascal, surround her and chase her this way. . . piggy, piggy."

Hak-su, following his mother's orders, went behind the wall of Mong-bun's house and chased out the pig. The villagers moved their feet in time to the striking of the gong by Yun. There among the others I, too, went back and forth but my heart wasn't in it. I was frustrated because I was unable to say what I was thinking inside.

The young men turned their attention to chasing after the

pig but that didn't keep them from watching the girls. Their frantic glances were more furtive than before. I felt utterly helpless. If the entire world had become an erupting volcano, then only would I have felt a sense of relief.

Round and Round the Pagoda

Harassed by the winds and rains of nearly three hundred years the house built on the slope of the mountain grew old and dilapidated. Since the house was on a siope it was hard to tell whether the land surrounding it was a mountain or a field. In the very beginning the man deliberately built the house in a place where there were many trees as if to remind his descendants that the planting of trees was one of the ways of observing family precepts. From that time on, generation after generation of ancestors had followed the leading of their forefather.

The trees were by no means planted haphazardly. At the advent of every new life, a male that is, a tree was planted to celebrate the event. It was not apparent whether the dream of the forebearer who had planted the first trees seeking to give eternal lasting prosperity to his descendants had come true. The old house after three hundred years of wind and rain only made the decrepit Poryon-hwa seem more desolate.

The cuckoo and other flying creatures came in season, each with its own song. The trees not only called for the mighty wind but when it was time for the heavy growth of leaves to fall they let go of them like a sudden shower. The sound of the melting of the snow which had clung to the branches was like footsteps. Poryon-hwa could hardly stand the loneliness.

She had reached the ripe old age of eighty-five. Although her given name was Poryon at the temple she was called by her Buddhist name, Poryon-hwa. Her father gave her the name Poryon and Monk Kag-il, the resident monk of Songam Temple, gave her the other. After all, it was only a matter of adding hwa* to her original name. When she reached fifty, as if to signify that her youth had passed, Monk Kag-il said that it was time now to change her name.

Since she had a Buddhist name it would appear that she was a firm believer but her father who was completely steeped in Chinese studies had not been in favor of her going to the temple. In addition he was so absorbed in teaching Chinese to his cherished only daughter that she had no time to play at the temple with the village children. This was how she spent her childhood.

Upon her father's death she went to the temple two or three times with her grandmother. Then when she married she went with her in-laws, but that only in order to show the proper respect. For a long time now she had been going to the temple to bow before Buddha but from beginning to end she was unable to accept the Buddhist doctrine for herself. Who knows whether or not this was due to her father's influence. It is true that she went because she felt utterly devoted to Monk Kag-il, whom she greatly esteemed.

So much for that. First, let's start in the beginning. She was well on into her eighties, about eighty-five or so, and it

* hwa : a word meaning flower, often used as part of a girl's name.

might be said that she had lived a long life. Her life had been difficult so there was no way of knowing whether or not that long life had been monotonous or not.

Three days after her birth her mother died. A tiny baby who had just lost its mother could do nothing but cry so that she was carried on her grandmother's back from then until she was four years old. As soon as she began to talk, and while she was still on her grandmother's back, her father began teaching her the first thousand Chinese characters. When she had memorized almost half that number she came down off her grandmother's back. Poryon learned mathematics and about the time that she was studying the Analects of Confucius she lost her father also. Once again she started to cry day and night. However, this time her crying was different from the time when she was a tiny baby and knew nothing about the world. No sooner had her father died than her aunt came to live with her. Her aunt said that no doubt the reason her parents had died was because she carried on in such a sorrowful way. Or, she would blurt out to Poryon, "My goodness, so tiresome." Or, "What a frightening sound!" shaking her head back and forth.

Poryon did not marry when she reached marriageable age because her grandmother couldn't bear the thought of her leaving. It was not until her grandmother was on her death bed that she called Min Song-hwan, who lived in the village, to her bedside. Her dying wish was that he arrange a marriage between her grand-daughter and one of his sons. At that time Poryon was eighteen and Min's son was seventeen. Min Song-hwan was not only a friend of her dead son, Poryon's father, but in addition his family had a good reputation in the village. Since the Min family was well off who knows whether her grandmother had been waiting for a proposal of marriage all along. According to her dying wish, the wedding came off as arranged, and Poryon went to live as a bride in the Min's house. But, strangely enough, misfortune continued to follow her. The young couple had been married but three months when the groom, without any sign of having been in poor health, died. Shortly afterwards her father-in-law who had taken to his bed in grief after his son's death passed away only to be followed to the other world by her mother-in-law.

Poryon did not cry remembering what her aunt had said about her parent's death being the result of her carryings on. The memory of her aunt's admonition came back to her like streaks of driving rain and she was embarrassed and frightened.

At the present time Poryon-hwa lived alone. Su-dong's mother lived in the lower part of the house so that in this old run-down, large house there were only these two old people.

Formerly the lower part of the house had been the servants' quarters. On the morning of Hyŏng-o's birth, Poryon's father-in-law planted a tree in the middle of the courtyard in honor of this grandson, the child of his own devoted dead son. Then he called Su-dong's grandfather and told him that the master-servant relationship was ended. Naturally, it followed that the name of the servants' quarters had also been changed. The reason that Su-dong's mother was now living alone was because of an incident which happened during the Korean War. Su-dong was forced to hide because of something he had done and he finally disappeared with his wife and child.

Poryon-hwa's great grand-daughter named Chae-sil was now twenty-three years old. She went to Seoul to attend college and after her graduation remained in Seoul and did not return to her home.

Chae-sil's father, Tak, Poryon-hwa's grandson, went into the volunteer army as soon as hostilities broke out on June 25. However, when he left home he didn't say that he was planning to join the army, but instead, said that he was going to bring back his father who had already gone north.

When Poryon-hwa heard what Tak intended to do she was frightened and her whole body shook. She cried out in a loud voice, "You're going to bring back your father? How are you going to bring him back? Why that's more than 90 thousand ri away."

Tak replied, "Grandmother, that's a thing of the past, to talk about that many li. Why with the 38th parallel it's only a short way now."

Tak talked with such assurance in his voice that Poryon-hwa answered, "He's coming, he's coming, so your father is that close. Of course you must go and get him. We can all live together, that's the way it should be. What's living like this anyway? One has to see each other in order to live right. One has to live together. That's how it should be." It was as if her son had already returned, and as she talked on and on her heart was filled with happiness.

Early the next morning after Tak left, the old barmaid who ran the wine shop in front of the railroad station came carrying a small baby in her arms. She carefully put the baby down in front of Poryon-hwa. Poryon-hwa's heart fell. This was not the first time she had gone through this same experience. Although this was the first time to see this old woman in person, since the town was small, Poryon-hwa not only knew that she sold wine at a place in front of the station but that a prostitute worked at her bar. Poryon-hwa was speechless. She just stood there and with her eyes asked the old woman why she had come. Without saying a word the woman took a sealed letter from the waist of her trousers and gave it to Poryon-hwa.

She recognized Tak's handwriting immediately. Tak often sent her by letter the things he should have told her in person.

"Grandmother, forgive me. Please don't say anything but take care of this child. I wasn't able to tell you myself and I really did intend to do so up until this very day but now I am letting you know. Although I know this sounds like I'm telling you a story I think that in this present situation I can escape. From the time that father ran away to the north our family has been known as the family of someone who fled north and we have suffered much because of this. You know for yourself how ruthless they are to destroy any groups, or any young people's organizations, and the like. Grandmother, you know the great number of terrible things they do. It was when I was so frightened and depressed, trying to calm myself and doing anything to get myself out of this mess, that this happened. As for me, I wanted to follow your wishes that I marry well and I wanted to make you happy. But, this terrible thing which has come about in our country, I just don't have the guts to stay and face it. Grandmother, even though this child is not the baby of a girl with a good family, for the sake of your devoted son, my father's blood and mine, blood of your blood, have pity on this child and please raise her well. Grandmother, don't despise this grandson who has left you with this burden but instead wait for me because I intend to go and bring back my father. So goodbye. By the way, the mother of the child is not too bad looking. At least, she doesn't look like a male rooster. I wrote this so you could have a good laugh, Grandmother. The child's name is Hyŏn Chae-sil and she was born on June 10, 1950."

Without saying a word, Poryon-hwa went to the wardrobe and took quite a sum of money from the stack inside. As she gave the money to the old barwoman she told her to ask the mother of the baby to leave the village. The old woman put the money in a safe place inside of her pocket. Before leaving she told Poryon-hwa that the mother already talked about leaving for the sake of the baby's future.

After the old barwoman left Poryon-hwa opened the baby's diapers. Although she could guess by the baby's name and features, she deliberately took a look, just in case, if by some chance she might be wrong. As she guessed the baby did not have a penis. She covered up the baby's crotch and recalled an event which had happened more than twenty years ago.

She was looking at Tak's crotch. Even though the light was dim she could tell by the front of his protruding diapers that he had a penis. She cried aloud to Hyŏng-o who had gone to his room, "He's got a penis, a penis. . . ."

It was more like early spring than late winter. The night had quieted down when her son, Hyŏng-o, came into her room with a little baby in his arms. At first she didn't know what he was carrying and it wasn't until she looked at it that she discovered it was a newborn baby still covered with blood, wrapped in a blanket.

She asked him. "What in the world is this?"

He replied, "Mother, this is your grandson."

"My grandson?"

He told her not to ask any more questions as he went to his room.

Hyŏng-o was nineteen and a high school student when he struck his Japanese teacher with a desk and then beat him up. He was taken to the police station.

When did he have the time to get involved in this situation? He asked her not to question him any further but she wanted to ask about several other things. For example, how many days ago had the baby been born? And, also, what had happened to the baby's mother? On the way to his room he said that the baby was two days old and that the mother had died. That was all. He quickly stepped over the sill to his room.

Poryon-hwa didn't sleep a wink that night trying to figure out who was the mother of the baby. No matter how hard she tried she couldn't guess when it could have happened. He had spent four nights under detention at the police station when he hit and beat up his Japanese teacher. Other than that he hadn't been out of the house at night nor had he brought a girl home.

The next morning as soon as he was out of bed she was in

his room. She started by asking him if the baby's mother came from a good family.

"Mother, you saw her two times or so," he abruptly responded.

"When and where did I see her?" She urged him on, flailing at him with her hands.

"Wasn't it the year before last, in the winter, when I brought her twice, I mean at night."

"The winter before last?" She couldn't recall him having brought a girl home. She stared at him.

"The friend who came with the cape, that was. . . ." He didn't finish talking but laughed in embarrassment.

"You mean to say that was a girl?"

"Yes. We wanted to fool you, so she came in wearing my hat and my cape." When he finished saying this, he laughed loudly, but she could neither laugh nor cry.

It wasn't until after he told her this that she recalled several times the winter before when he brought home a young man, wearing a student's hat and a cape, who stayed overnight. Both times the student left early the next morning without eating breakfast. Each time she asked him why he sent his friend off before breakfast without feeding him. Since the friend left early she always said, "He should eat before you send him off. How can you just let him go like that?"

As she expected, because of this incident, Tak's mother was not a young woman from a good family. If she had grown up in a family with a good reputation she couldn't have dressed in men's clothes, gone home with a boy and then slept with him. It was obvious that Tak's mother was large for a girl. She was only eighteen but even so she looked like a full-grown young man and Hyŏng-o's clothes didn't look strange but fit as if they belonged to her. If she had appeared the least bit awkward who knows whether his mother would have suspected something. If one were to compare her with a rooster she would be one of the larger ones, and in no way would be mistaken for a hen. How could Poryon-hwa guess that she was a girl?

She asked him if it were really true that the mother had died. Without even a cloud of sadness passing over his face he said that was what she was to believe. He made no response when she continued to say that a mother who gives birth to a baby needs to stay alive in order to take care of the baby.

When Tak reached the right age it was due to this incident that she told him again and again that he must marry a young girl from a good family and also that she shouldn't be big like a rooster. This was the reason Tak wrote what he did at the end of the letter.

Less than three years after liberation, in 1947, Hyŏng-o went north. He was in the second year of middle school when he was taken into custody for hitting the teacher. From that time on he was on the black list. One incident followed another for which he was put in detention or prison so that in the end he was unable to finish school. He was in prison when liberation came. On that morning his mother cried mansei* as the prison gates were opened and the prisoners who were released came out. Although it was impossible to know who was who because of the beards that entirely covered their faces, the people embraced the prisoners and together yelled mansei at the top of their lungs. When Hyong-o actually recognized his mother and approached her she was so overjoyed that she didn't know whether it was from happiness or sadness.

From then he remained in Seoul and she kept worrying about him as he was continually on the move with his prison buddies. She worried about his health, too. However, she came to the conclusion that he was helping his country which was once again directing its own course. Then she felt better. She reasoned that there was nothing for which he

* mansei : cheers; hurrah.

could be put in chains again so it really didn't hurt him to be running around like this. While her mind was full of these worries, one day, to her horror, Hyŏng-o returned to the house in disguise.

Poryon-hwa shook like a leaf as she approached him and asked the meaning of this. Liberation had come, this was his country, and why was he in disguise? Hyŏng-o laughed and said that he was only killing time. Although he acted as if it were nothing significant, from that time until he eventually left for the north, he remained in hiding.

It was a night when only stars were twinkling here and there in the sky. Whatever the reason, a life together with her family was not to be. She breathed a heavy sigh. An endless, wide, green field spread out before her eyes. A sleek-bodied white colt without bridle or reins ran around on the green field flooded with sunlight. She, herself, ran out on the field in order to catch the white colt. The colt took flight, running feverishly. The colt ran and Poryon ran, too. She was unable to catch the bridleless colt. The colt disappeared. Poryon stretched out on the field and cried.

"Child, child, wake up." The sound of her mother-in-law's voice calling her awakened her, but she continued to cry.

"So you saw that character in your dreams. Save us, Goddess of Mercy."

"No, Mother," Poryon said, as she told her about her dream.

"My gracious. He didn't make paradise but instead is running round and round in hell. Have mercy, oh, merciful Buddha. Oh, Goddess of Mercy, save us."

Although it was apparent that her mother-in-law thought that the dream was about her son, Poryon interpreted it differently. Evidently her mother-in-law hadn't thought about the possibility of her son's seed having been planted in the womb of her daughter-in-law since he had died only three months after their wedding.

When Poryon gave birth to Hyŏng-o's child eight months

later, there was no doubt but that her dream had been one of conception. The next morning after Hyŏng-o's birth her father-in-law planted an elm tree in the center of the courtyard. The reason he planted an elm was because of its many spreading branches and abundant leaves. Her father-in-law passed away but the tree and Hyŏng-o grew together. The year that Hyŏng-o left home he was thirty-eight, and sure enough, as her father-in-law had predicted, the tree, after thirty-eight years, had spread out in every direction.

On the night that Hyŏng-o left, the elm, as if knowing that he had gone, with a great rustling sound dropped all of its leaves at one time. She wanted desperately to call out to him, or even to cry out to the Goddess of Mercy, but she kept silent. She controlled her feelings for she knew that if she opened her mouth the tears would gush out like water from a bursting dike. Once again she remembered what her aunt had said to her. Deep into the night she encircled the elm tree, again and again. The leaves fell around her, some landed on her head while others settled on her shoulders.

The next morning Poryon-hwa went off in the direction of Songam Temple. Whenever something disturbing happened it was her custom to go off to see Monk Kag-il. From the time when Hyong-o was taken in by the police for striking and beating his Japanese teacher she started this practice.

However, this was the first time since liberation that she had come to the temple. As soon as Monk Kag-il noticed her he wondered what had happened. Upon hearing her story all he did was to chant a prayer to Buddha.

Poryon-hwa couldn't understand his response and directly confronted him, saying. "There was no other way, what am I to do, I'm at my wit's end. I came because it seemed that all I could do was to come and see you, Monk Kag-il."

As before, Monk Kag-il said nothing but only kept on chanting his prayers.

Poryon-hwa left the monk and went outside in the direction of the pagoda which was next to the Chilsŏngkak* intending to circle it. Her reason for deciding to do this was because an old woman in mourning clothes had once told her that the short cut to getting one's wishes was to first circle the pagoda. She told Poryon-hwa that as a string is unwound from a spool so one's desires are as readily granted.

At that time Poryon was in mourning clothes and perhaps this was the reason that the old woman who was circling the pagoda stopped in her tracks and called Poryon to join her. One must start from the right side and go around all in one breath. She told Poryon to follow behind her and they circled once and then again. Suddenly Poryon, who was behind, found herself in front of the old woman. Although she circled two times in one breath she was still not out of breath. Was it because she was full of desire for Monk Kag-il? She was pregnant with Hyŏng-o, but still, she was faster than the old woman.

"Sister, let's go inside the temple." She stopped in her tracks and looked around to see Monk Kag-il with his hands folded together.

The sky was swaying, the bare trees were moving, and the main temple was weaving. As they all swayed together Poryon-hwa fell over. Monk Kag-il tried to pick her up and then called another priest. The two of them moved her to the back room where they put her down on the floor. It was the room to which Poryon-hwa always went when she came to the temple. Although the sunlight was faint it filled the room. Across the room, not only the nape of Monk Kag-il's neck but his whole body was steeped in the sunlight. She gazed at his long, white neck. Was it the faint light which made him look so forlorn and made the heavy wrinkles of flesh look as big as life? Was this the reason that the long, white neck had become a big lump and appeared to have shortened?

* Chilsŏngkak : a shrine to the Dipper.

"Sister, shut your eyes and rest." Monk Kag-il said to Poryon-hwa who was looking him up and down. She shut her eyes.

Quite some time after closing her eyes she asked him, "Monk Kag-il, if you cross the 38th parallel is it true that you can't come back?"

"Why not? Why can't you come back? If the 38th parallel is opened then you can come back."

"When will it be opened?"

"It will be opened, of course. It has to be. One can't live otherwise. No, lie down and rest a bit and then let's go up to the temple. Have mercy on us, oh merciful Buddha."

Although she was still dizzy she got up in order to go to the temple. She bowed over and over again before Buddha as she rubbed her hands together begging for the opening of the 38th parallel. This was the first time that she had prayed so earnestly. In fact, it was the first time that she had even uttered these words out loud.

Poryon-hwa first discovered Monk Kag-il at the temple altar when the mass was said for her dead husband on the 49th day memorial after his death. They had been married for only a short time. Was that the reason that his face wasn't familiar to her? All she could remember was the flapping of the hem of his green silk coat. She suppressed the deep sorrow she felt while the prayer mass was chanted.

> Creation is ever changing;
> Only death can overcome the cares and the worries of this world.
> Human beings know happiness only in the other world.
> Death must come in order for happiness to become a reality.

The monk who was conducting the service chanted along with the playing of the instruments which accompanied the altar service, the cymbal, the handbell, the drum, the gong and the horn. How was it that one person's voice could be heard ringing so clearly amidst all of that commotion?

Unexpectedly she stopped bowing in front of the statue of Buddha and turned her shoulders in the direction of the clear ringing sound. The April sun flowing in through the large open door made golden waves roll inside of the sanctuary. In this setting the young monk with the long, white neck was sitting. The sunbeams shining on that long, white neck blinded the eyes.

If it hadn't been for the sputtering noise of the candles who knows whether or not she would have been able to take her eyes off of that long, white neck. The longer she looked the more difficult it became. The sound of the burning candles seemed exactly like the clicking of the tongue and this made Poryon immediately straighten her shoulders and turn around. She turned toward the statue of Buddha and lifted her two hands high in the air in preparation for bow. His eyes were focused right on her and it seemed as if he was eyeing her with disapproval.

"It won't do you any good to look at him. Besides, that's an evil thing to do."

Poryon was thrown into a state of confusion. She became intent on chanting the Amitabha rosary, "Save me merciful Buddha."

When she was finished saying the prayers for the dead she went outside. The temple grounds were flooded with sunshine and on the one side the peach and the apricot blossoms were glittering like the sunset. At that precise moment the cuckoo could be heard from the nearby mountain singing at the top of its voice. She became suddenly aware of her alienation from this world.

It was the fourth of July in 1972. She was taking an afternoon nap when she was awakened by someone moving outside of the sliding door. It was Su-dong's mother.

After checking to be sure that Poryon-hwa was awake she

carefully slid open the door and said. "They say we're going to be united, Ma'am."

"What? What's that you just said? We're going to be united? You mean, the north and south are going to get together?"

"Yes, that's right. A little while ago Kwi-buk's father came and he asked me to tell you."

"Well, if that's true why didn't you wake me up? Where did he hear that news?"

"He said that he heard it on the radio. They said that some high official had been up to Pyŏngyang and back. Kwi-buk's father said he was going to tell several other families and that he would be right back."

As she was talking he returned and said, "Grandmother, why are you just standing there? Why aren't you dancing? Your son will come back, and Tak will come, and . . . ."

"Is that really true?"

"Of course, it's the truth. Why didn't our most important people go up there?"

"Really, did they go farther than 90 thousand li? Are you telling me the truth? Did those people really go up there?" She pricked up her ears and opened her eyes wide.

"Yes, Granny. That's the way they announced it on the radio."

"Well, if that's the case what do you mean, dance? Why I'd even walk upside down on my hands."

"I've been to all of the other houses and no one is as happy as you are Granny."

"It's just like a dream to think of seeing my kids coming, a dream."

No sooner did Poryon-hwa stop talking than Su-dong's mother, who was standing beside her, suddenly burst into tears. She cried like a child. They turned their heads in her direction. Both of them knew why she was crying and they said nothing.

Poryon-hwa said to Kwi-buk's father, "Don't you have to

go?" He left.

"Don't cry. Let's ask around to see if we can't locate him. They say you can find people by advertising in the newspapers. We've done nothing about it for twenty years, so I don't know. But let's ask Kwi-buk's father to put an ad in the paper. Stop your crying."

"Thank you, Ma'am."

"Why do you keep on calling me Ma'am? Why do you talk like that? If my father-in-law knew he would turn over in his grave. Before you came here as a bride, on the morning of Hyŏng-o's birth, my father-in-law planted a tree for him and then he called your father-in-law and told him from that day on they were no longer master and servant."

"Yes, I know that, Ma'am. But, even so when your family returns what will they think? What right does a criminal like me have to live here?"

"Criminal? Who called you that? Let's just forget it. Let's do as we used to do and you just call me mother."

"How can a criminal dare to do that?" The tears that were bottled up inside of her suddenly flowed as she cried louder.

"Listen to me. Stop that kind of talk, and quit your crying right this minute. I won't stand for it. Crying makes bad things happen. Stop it."

"If that kid only hadn't gone crazy, I would be taking care of you and . . ." she sobbed on in a muffled voice.

"It wasn't Su-dong who went crazy, it's these times we live in. Stop your crying. It only hurts him so just quit it."

As soon as Poryon-hwa said that crying would hurt Su-dong she stopped.

Although this little village was a mere 50 ri from Seoul, as soon as they heard that the communist soldiers were driven out and that the United Nations forces had entered Seoul, all kinds of confusion erupted. An autonomous government was organized as well as other groups. Su-dong became active in the government group. Poryon-hwa was taken before each of these groups, the government group, the branch groups and the private ones, for questioning.

During the upset Poryon-hwa heard from one of Hyŏng-o's friends that her son would return. This friend had been close to Hyŏng-o since the Japanese days and they had suffered much together. They had been released from prison together at liberation and because of this relationship she felt as if she were seeing her son when she met him. It made her very happy so that she took him in, gave him a place to sleep, fed him and washed his clothes. She thought that they would all live together when Hyŏng-o returned. However, this friend began to bring one or two friends home with him until there were twenty of them in all.

With the infant Chae-sil on her back she picked the tender turnips which her son had enjoyed eating. It was hard enough work to prepare a jar of kimchi* every day to say nothing of all of that laundry. She hardly had time to sleep at night. Then, too, wherever she was taken for questioning they asked her why she didn't know enough to be embarrassed to be taking care of the grandchild of a turncoat, and she, herself, almost on her death bed. Besides other things they accused her of being so delirious with happiness when the communist soldiers came that she danced for joy.

One day when she returned home after undergoing this harsh treatment, crying noises and a loud pounding-like clamor coming from inside of the house met her ears. She hurried inside only to see Su-dong and his mother in a desperate struggle beside the wardrobe. The door had been ripped off and had fallen down. Poryon-hwa knew immediately that it was because the property deed was inside of the wardrobe. As soon as Su-dong saw her he picked up the club that was standing in the corner of the room and sprang upon her with the swinging club. Su-dong's mother stepped in front of Poryon-hwa, blocking her, so that Su-dong hit his

* kimchi : a food made from cabbage, or other vegetables, with red pepper, garlic, scallions, ginger and fish, allowed to ripen and eaten as a daily staple with rice and other foods.

mother instead. At the sound of her screaming to please spare her life, Su-dong took to his heels and ran away.

From that time on his mother's right arm was useless. That arm was left to hang just as it was for twenty years. The club was the one that Su-dong had made out of hard birch wood and given to Poryon-hwa for her protection. She kept it standing in a corner of the room.

When Kwi-buk's father came the next morning he said that one of the men in the village obstinately opposed a newspaper advertisement to locate Su-dong. This man wanted to know why in the world they wanted to find some communist rascal. Poryon-hwa's whole body stiffened when Kwi-buk's father related this without any thought of what she might think. What about her children? Is this the way they thought about them? She began to worry.

She continued pulling up the onions and planted half of the onion patch with turnip seed. She repaired a corner of the gate which had fallen down when it was hit by a bomb. She busied herself in making preparations to welcome her son and grandson. After the gate was hit again in the January 4th retreat she left it as it was. A number of Chinese soldiers were observed from the air as they were coming into her yard and the United Nations soldiers dropped a bomb.

Neither her son nor her grandson returned. The rumors about Su-dong were disturbing. It was said that he had gone to a deserted island with only a couple of houses on it; or that he was wandering around the streets of Seoul in a disturbed mental state; or that his wife had remarried or that she had drowned.

Again the two old people became as quiet as death, both on the inside and the outside. In this way day and night passed, over and over again. As usual, the trees came into bud. The leaves appeared and the leaves fell. The cuckoo and the magpie came, as well as the other flying things, each one making its own song. The snows came. The moon came up. There were times when the moonlight made the whole body numb.

The days passed like this until one morning Chae-sil appeared with a young man who she said was her fiance. Poryon-hwa was out in the back tending the garden when Su-dong's mother called out to say that Chae-sil had come.

"Oh, is that right, Chae-sil's here?" She called out in a louder voice than Su-dong's mother had used.

It had been almost two years since she had seen her great-grand daughter. If her legs had still been strong she would already have gone to Seoul and back several times. But, for three years or so, because her legs had shriveled, she was unable to walk straight. She was waiting for news of Chae-sil. quickly looked back over her shoulder in the direction outside of the gate and urged someone to come in.

"Did you come with a friend? Well, if you came together tell your friend to come in."

As soon as he heard, a tall, slender young man came and stood inside of the gate.

Poryon-hwa said to herself, "Look at that, not you, too." She felt like the bottom had dropped out and she grabbed her arms in fright.

"Well, let's at least go into the house." She urged them in and as soon as they went in she closed the sliding door tightly.

Chae-sil pushed open the door as she said, "Grandmother, why did you close the door when it is so hot?"

"I'm embarrassed."

"What? Embarrassed?"

"How come is it that you bring a young man when you've been gone so long? What is this?"

"Grandmother, stop that. We're engaged."

"You're engaged? How did you get here from the station? Did you walk?"

"Well, if we didn't walk, did we fly?"

"Then the whole village had a look at you."

"So what if they did. Grandmother, you're always worried about what other people are thinking. It's time you knew that in today's world boys and girls walk down the street arm in arm."

"I don't know about Seoul, maybe you can do that and no one thinks anything of it, but here it's different."

"If it's different, so what? Why in this little hole . . . Mr. Yu, you should bow to my grandmother. She's my great-grandmother. Grandmother, come and let him pay his respects."

As he bowed she kept thinking that she didn't want him to but since she was unable to say anything she merely accepted it.

"The people here don't know that you're engaged so let's have another engagement party. Let's invite all of the people in the village and close by, kill a pig, make rice cakes and have a big party."

"Again these country folks, why?"

"I don't know what you think, but I'm afraid of them and they make me feel embarrassed."

Poryon-hwa was barely able to talk because her chin was quivering. It was a small village with about two hundred houses, including the surrounding area. Rumors were like boiling water. In addition, the children in her family, beginning with Hyŏng-o, then Tak, and now Chae-sil, too, had gone to Seoul. Chae-sil stayed in Seoul after finishing college even though she didn't have a job. Already they were being criticized because Chae-sil hadn't come back.

"Stop that and let's get down to business," said the young man, who up until this time hadn't said a word.

Poryon-hwa was taken aback at his impertinence and could only stare at his mouth.

"Grandmother, we're going to get married at the end of the month."

"Where?"

"At the Changan Hotel in Seoul."

"Well, if you're having it in Seoul that means I won't be able to come. Because of my legs . . . ."

"If you just give us your blessing that's good enough. You pay for the wedding and buy us a place to live in."

Poryon-hwa felt empty as if she were no longer needed. "Goodness me. Just because I'm old and about to die you don't treat me like a person."

"Grandmother, what are you saying? If I didn't think of you as a human being would I've come so that you could see my fiance, and also to talk with you about my wedding?"

"Anyway, let's forget the past. They say that soon our country will be united and then your grandfather will return and your father, also. They're all coming back. Let's have the wedding then."

"Reunification? Why that's only a dream? It's a long ways off, don't you know that?"

"You leave right now. Get right out. I thought I'd raised the child of a man but instead I've raised a savage. Get out!"

She was unable to suppress her anger. She forgot about her bad legs as she ran to the other end of the room like a bullet shot from a gun. She took the club that was propped up in the corner and the noise of the swinging club was like the whirring sound of a whirlwind. Blue sparks fell from her eyes.

The young man, in one stride on those long legs was the first to jump over the doorsill, followed by Chae-sil. They went down to the stones in front of the house before they turned around to look back into the room. They said that they'd be back in a couple of days with a lawyer as it was necessary in order to transfer the property. They added that the property had to be transferred before her death in order for only a small inheritance tax to be levied on the property.

After they left, Su-dong's mother, her right arm hanging by her side, came to the room and stretched her neck to peek inside. In the glaring sunlight she looked shabby.

"Why are you just standing there like that? Did you think that there was something to look at?"

As soon as Poryon-hwa stopped talking Su-dong's mother

vanished like the gentle falling of dry, dead leaves. Shortly after, for no reason at all, Poryon-hwa gently collapsed on her side. She was like a balloon from which the air had all escaped.

She saw Monk Kag-il. He had gone up on the mountain behind Songam Temple. At first it seemed so close that she could touch it with her hand. Suddenly a dense fog appeared from nowhere. The fog was so heavy that it was impossible to tell the difference between the mountains, the rocks, the trees and the hills. Monk Kag-il was invisible, too, except for the corner of his robe which appeared and disappeared by turns. As she reached out to grab hold of the corner of his robe it, too, disappeared into the fog and was gone.

From then on she was ill. While she was sick she heard about the death of the grandmother of Hyong-o's childhood friend, Kwi-buk. Her body felt as if it were flowing away deep down into the ground. As the feeling intensified when her eyes were shut she struggled hard to keep them open. However, she was unaware when they closed automatically.

"How could it be that a person who was full of life die like that? Why only yesterday I went and had a little talk and now you say that she's gone?" Poryon-hwa protested to Su-dong's mother who told her the news.

"They said that she lay down after eating breakfast, and of course, she closed her eyes. You can't tell with the old ones. They can eat and just pass on."

"If that's so how can the children watch at the death bed? Oh, yes, a bit earlier you called Kwi-buk's grandmother an old woman, didn't you?" She questioned Su-dong's mother for some time in this manner.

"Yes, Ma'am, we were the same age. We would've been sixty-four this year."

"Why in no time at all you're that old? How did time slip by so quickly?"

The pretty figure of a young girl appeared before Poryon-hwa's eyes. Words couldn't express how sweet and tender the face was. At the time Su-dong's mother was carrying her own grandchild on her back. Poryon-hwa had asked her whether it was proper to call someone a child who was caring for her own grandchild? Su-dong's mother laughed like a child, and told Poryon-hwa to call her that as long as she wished. Besides, Su-dong's mother said that she liked being called a child.

The two of them often sat talking under Hyong-o's tree because the wooden frame bed was there. The day after Hyong-o left the two of them together, lifted and moved the wooden frame bed to Hyong-o's tree. At the time Poryonhwa was not old and Su-dong's mother was young.

"You grew a lot during that time, didn't you?" Su-dong's mother said as she stared up at the elm tree.

"Do you know how old this tree is?"

"Of course. Hyong-o, I mean your son, that's right, the morning of his birth it was planted. So it should be about thirty-eight years old, shouldn't it? We grew up together so he and I are the same age."

"Listen, as I used to call you child, you called Hyong-o by his name. Please don't call him my son. I like to hear his name. That's what I miss."

"Oh, all right. Of course, the tree took after him and was strong and sturdy. Did you know how short his temper was? He hit me a lot."

The two not only attended primary school together but since there were no other children in the village they were always together. It didn't seem to matter that they were not of the same sex.

"I couldn't stand up to him. At school the other children didn't meddle with him. They couldn't do anything to him. One time when I had had it I scratched him so hard he bled. As he was wiping off the blood he told me not to tell you. I said to him, 'You mean, you aren't going to tell your mother that I scratched you until the blood came?' And, he pounded my face with his fists. I really screamed. My mother heard us from inside the house and called out, 'So you're at it again.' She scolded Hyŏng-o. He was so afraid that I might tell her that I had scratched him and his face was bleeding. In a low voice he said to me, 'If you tell I'll kill you.' I have such fond memories of him. If he only hadn't left, it's really too bad."

"He was like that from the moment I dreamed that I was pregnant with him. The horse had no reins or bridle and I couldn't catch it. I only gave him birth. He ran off and I lost him."

"Well, of course, that's the way he left, but you don't know, he might come back as easily."

Poryon-hwa, who had been reliving the past, jumped up with a start, not at all like the sick person she was, and sliding the door wide open looked down at Kwi-buk's house. Although the houses were some distance apart because there was nothing between them and since Poryon-hwa's house was high on a hill, all was visible at the lower house. It was the same with sounds. The noises that came from that house were so clear they could be held in the palm of one's hand. The smoke from the chimney went straight up into the sky. The moon shining on the roof and the smoke made the whole place look like a picture.

"How could she die so easily? Surely she had something to say. How could that be?" abruptly she mumbled over and over to herself.

As soon as Su-dong's mother returned from the funeral she asked her if she had died without saying one word, even at the very last.

"What would she have said, after all a person who is dying?"

"Yes, but, surely you have something you want to say before you die."

"When was there time to say something? She died in her sleep, after all. . . ."

"If she knew she were about to die surely she would have had something to say. It's so frustrating." Poryon-hwa reached out for Su-dong's mother's good arm and grabbed it with both of her hands in an attempt to relieve her deep frustration.

"Of course, all people are going to die and don't they have something they want to say? Yes, they do. Well, the reason I am thinking about death is because Kwi-buk's grandmother has gone. Up until now I've been living never even thinking about death. I've spent all of my time and energy on waiting and haven't had one moment to think about this kind of thing. My eyes and ears are constantly turned to the outside. I mean, my whole body, all of it. When the magpie cries I look out at the noise it makes. I open the door at the sound of the wind. When we heard the news that our country might be united it seemed as if I could hear their laughing voices outside the door and that they were on their way in. That's why I haven't thought about dying. I haven't had one minute to do so."

"Mother, someday those two men will come swaggering through that gate. You just eat and keep up your strength. Isn't that what you have to do so you will be able to see them again?"

"Yes, you are right, of course, I have to eat and keep up my strength."

"Shall I bring you something, say some rice gruel?"

"No, but would you go and get Monk Kag-il?"

"Why do you want him so suddenly?"

"It's already long since that I should've gone to see him but I couldn't leave the house since I didn't know when our country would be united, today or tomorrow, or just when. And, besides, the mountain path has so many ups and downs that it's hard for me. So I haven't gone. I know you're tired but would you mind going?"

Su-dong's mother stared hard at the reclining face of Poryon-hwa for several moments and then answered, "Sure, I'll go."

Although she went outside she stood beside the sliding doors because she felt uneasy and wondered whether she shouldn't first heat some rice gruel and give it to her before leaving. Or, should she get someone to come and stay with her. She might get lonely. However, Poryon-hwa had only urged her to go and return, nothing else.

After Su-dong's mother left, Poryon-hwa, her mind clear as a bell, thought over what she would talk about with Monk Kag-il.

"Let's plan to give the onion patch in the back to Su-dong's mother. She really can't do any heavy farming with that useless arm and even if Su-dong returns they can live on that."

She hesitated about Chae-sil until she unexpectedly thought about the letter that Tak had written and left for her.

"Grandmother, your son, my father, is blood of your blood, as is this child. So please take good care of her."

She heard his voice again, begging her, and she decided to give Chae-sil enough to live on.

"The rest that's left, the rest of it. . . ." As she repeated this over and over, her voice blurred and as it faded away her eyes closed of their own accord. Then the tears started to flow. Like a dike that had burst, the tears that she had held back all this time because it wasn't right to cry, began to fall. However, the tears didn't last very long.

Her tears stopped when she began to circle the pagoda. She was not alone. Hyong-o was there, as well as Tak, Monk Kag-il, and Chae-sil, too. None of them had changed. Monk Kag-il looked exactly the same as he had on that first day when she saw him for the first time. That long white neck was the same. Hyŏng-o was wearing a cape and looked like he did on the day he left to go and bring back his father.

Poryon-hwa was in the lead. She looked behind and told the others they must go to the right and make one circle all in one breath in order for the pagoda to fulfill their wishes. This was exactly what the old woman in mourning clothes had told her. Poryon-hwa started out with all of them following behind. One circle in one breath; but though she did two circles in one breath she was still not out of breath.

The blue outstretched sky was swelling like waves above her head. The paulownia tree was spinning. The bodhi tree, full of blooming flowers, was weaving. The peach and the apricot trees were moving, too. As the wind blew, the petals of the flowers scattered. They fell like snow on their heads and settled on their shoulders. Some fell to the ground. A carefree smile formed on her lips, and the face of Poryon-hwa was sealed forever in a calm expression of peace.

The Moon and the Crab's Legs

by Hwang Sun-won
translated by Edward W. Poitras

The little crab was always happy. He liked to play with his friends on the soft moss which covered the rocks. Together they loved to bask in the bright sunshine which warmed the sand on the river's edge. As they soaked up the sun they blew bubbles which in turn caught the light making a beautiful prismlike rainbow.

The little crab enjoyed going into the water under the water lilies and watching the fish swim back and forth beneath him. How could there be so many different kinds of fish? The round, wide carp, the very flat fish, the slender flying fish, the catfish with the fleshy back and sides, and the catfish with the long snout and a very large mouth. All the while he was watching the fish, a school of minnows kept biting at him with their little mouths. He paid no attention to them except when one tried to peck at his eyes. When he raised his pinchers, pretending to pinch them, they quickly disappeared.

Paying no heed to the passing of time, he played this same game over and over again. He was happy.

One day he shed his shell. The new shell had been forming inside of the old one and the water which touched this new, soft shell felt ticklish and lively. As he came out of his old shell his movements were slow and unsteady. He could not remember when he had had such a satisfied feeling. Although he was no different than before, his old familiar surroundings looked different.

Right at that moment a baby turtle happened to pass by and seeing the little crab walking along he said, "You idiot! You can't even walk sideways properly."

The baby crab thought about this for a long time. What was the turtle talking about? Then understanding what the turtle meant, he watched closely as the turtle walked. Carefully he started walking. It was true. His walking was strange.

He sunk into a hole and tried to think. He thought and thought. "Why is it that I can only walk sideways? Even though I can't swim lightly to and fro as the fish do, why can't I walk any other way but sideways?" He was ashamed of himself.

Finally, he decided to go and ask the old grandfather crab. The old crab was speechless for a moment, and then with a forced laugh questioned, "Are you the only one?"

The little crab hadn't thought about that. But, then he asked, "Yes, but why is it that all of us crabs can only walk sideways?"

"Well, all of our ancestors did. Like father like son."

The little crab was not satisfied by this answer, so he went to find another grandfather crab.

This grandfather crab, immediately upon hearing the baby crab's question, retorted, "What kind of talk is that? Go and play with your friends." The baby crab was getting ready to say something when the grandfather crab grabbed him roughly by the shell with his huge legs and turned him over on his back.

After a long struggle his fragile body righted itself. No sooner had he turned himself over then the grandfather crab flipped him over again. Over and over again. The baby crab struggling to turn himself over, only to be flipped upside down again by the old crab. Over and over until the little crab completely exhausted, fell on his back with his belly-button up in the air and broke into sobs.

The grandfather crab, without even offering to help him get up, turned around and disappeared into his hole.

The little crab was frightened by the old crab. He began to see the world as an unfriendly place. He stopped crying and started to walk toward the stream, to the place where it began. The soft tips of his legs smarted and tingled and became sore, but he walked on. He wanted to be all alone in a far away place.

How far had he come? He reached a place where there was a luxuriant thick growth of pussy willows near the water. This seemed like a good place to live alone. In this deserted spot he dug a hole for his house next to the stump of one of the pussy willows. Exhausted he dropped off into a deep sleep.

In the middle of the night he was awakened by someone brushing into him. He opened his eyes.

"Please, let me sleep here," said a young lady eel.

"Don't you have a house?"

"I hate the rocks. Let me stay here with you."

The lady eel could not be still. She moved her back up and down and her slippery, sticky body continually rubbed the crab until finally he said, "Can't you be still?"

"Yes I'll try," she answered.

The next morning she left. Late that night she returned again. Like the night before she moved all night long.

The baby crab could stand it no longer. "Don't touch me," he said.

The young lady eel, behaving like a spoiled child, retorted, "Do I bother you that much?"

The crab was dumbfounded when she added, "Stop talking like that. Take your pinchers and scratch my back." She bent her back in front of him.

He decided to give her a good scare and prepared to pinch her hard with his claws. However, his claws only slipped off her slippery back.

The eel, giggling in a teasing manner, begged him to pinch her hard, one more time. The crab, moving to one side, made his body small and stayed awake all night. He was unable to sleep and decided to move from that place in the morning.

Once again he started to walk until he came to a fork in the stream. The mountain stood directly ahead of him. To the left, along the edge of the flat plain which bordered the mountains, ran the main branch of the stream while on the right the smaller branch followed the edge of the mountains. He walked into the smaller stream.

He had not gone far before the stream began to narrow. The sand in the bottom of the stream was gradually replaced by stones. At last he heard the sound of clear, clean, cold water as it flowed along the gorge. As night was falling he found a big rock and crawled under it only to be kicked several times. Several animals seemed to be taking turns kicking him.

He tried another rock. Again the same. He was kicked by some crayfish and sent out of the hole.

He was forced to sleep under the stars. Hunched up and looking up at the stars he fell asleep.

Early the next morning, once again he started going upward. He had not gone far before the sound of falling water became louder and louder. The water was falling from a steep place and cascading down the mountain.

He went closer and crawled into the water at the bottom of the falls. The water falling directly on his back felt cool. He stayed for a long time in the water until he felt something falling on his back. They were small fish. The fish were trying to jump to the top of the falls. They exerted a great amount of energy only to fall short of the top and end up back where they had started.

Over and over they jumped. As he carefully watched the falling water, he noticed that occasionally one of the fish made it to the top.

"I think that I will try once, too," he said to himself.

He started to climb up the falls behind the water. It was not an easy job. Exerting all his strength he managed to almost reach the top where the falls were strongest. The force of the water sent him back down to the bottom. He failed as often as he tried. At times he did not get as far as he had in his first try before he slipped and fell down again. Night was falling. Completely exhausted the crab gave up.

There was no place to make a house. He could not ask the crayfish to let him sleep in their house. Wherever he went or whatever he tried to do, nothing had turned out as he had planned. He gave up, letting the water take him where it willed.

The thought of his failures filled his breast so that he felt no pain even when his soft body bounded against the rocks in the stream. The awkward appearance he made lying on his back, kicking his legs in the air, grew and grew in his imagination.

Returning to his birth place he found a peaceful place to sleep. All seemed changed and nothing was like he had remembered. He no longer got a thrill in playing on the moss covered rocks with his friends, or basking in the sun on the bank of the river. Nor did he go into the water to watch the fish darting to and fro or to let the minnows playfully nip at him.

As far as possible, he decided not to make friends with anyone. More than anyone else he vowed to avoid the old crab and to live in a place where he would never have to meet him again.

Although food was plentiful he became thinner and thinner. One night he went into the sorghum field by the side of the river and crawled up on an ear of sorghum. From time to time the wind blew harder and as the stalks of grain moved in the wind the leaves rustled. As the eastern sky lightened the moon started to rise. It was the first time that he had seen the big, white moon. It looked as if a big hole had been punched in the sky. If only he could live in a hole in the sky just like that one!

The leaves of the sorghum made a rustling sound in the wind. Forgetting even to eat the grain, lost in a trance, he stared at the moon, and loosing his grip on the leaf he fell head over heels to the ground. His whole body was dull with pain from the fall so that for a long time he could not move. It seemed as if voices were coming at him from all directions, making fun of him.

Daily the water became clearer and more transparent. The skin of the different kinds of fish became shiny. The crabs, too, started to fill out and take on a sturdy look except the baby crab who looked shabby and miserable.

While crawling on the river bottom, all by himself, the little crab discovered an earthworm slowly wiggling back and forth. He began to eat the worm when, for no reason, the worm gave a jerk and the crab with the half-eaten earthworm in his mouth suddenly jerked upward with the worm. As he flew through the water he felt just like the fish swimming in the river.

Coming out of the river so suddenly the sun momentarily blinded his eyes. He saw the man standing on the edge of the river. The shock made him let go of the worm as he had landed upside down on the edge of the embankment. The man, reaching out his hand, leaped toward the crab. Frightened, the baby crab sprang up with a jerk and ran to one side, then nimbly changing directions he ran into the water. Even in his wildest imagination he had not dreamed that he could move so expertly.

"Oh, shucks, missed him," grumbled the man.

Deep down in the water the little crab regaining his breath managed a smile. He had not smiled for a long time. If he had been unable to walk sideways he would have been caught. He recalled the time when the old crab had tipped him over again and again. At the time he thought that the old crab was tormenting him. Suddenly he knew better. Once more he smiled.

One day that winter, before the crab was preparing to go to the place where he would spend the winter, he lost all of his legs at one time to a man who was trying to catch a crab. There was no mistake, he was nothing but a stone.

Even though he could not move he could think. He was able to remember more clearly now than he had been able to before he lost his legs. Once again in his memory he brushed against the soft moss that covered the rock. Each bubble that he made created a dazzling rainbow of color which shone again in his memory. Under the water lilies the shape and form of each fish swimming beneath him became clear and distinct before his eyes. He thought about the water fall in the valley of the upper stream which he had tried to crawl up only to fall back again. Again he had failed. His exhausted form appeared before his eyes. Once again he recalled how he had finally given up his body to the stream.

All of these events he saw now more clearly than at the time they had happened.

Did I really fail? He thought over and over again. Did I really fail?

After the man had pulled off his legs and gone, a slow, steady rain started to fall on the empty stretch of sand outside of the wide hole. Night had come. From inside his hole he heard the sound of the crabs going by on their way to the place where the river flowed into the sea, the sign of the approaching winter.

One of them came into hole and said, "Everyone is going to the river bottom. Aren't you going, too?"

It was the old grandfather crab who had turned him upside down.

Without saying a word the baby crab kept his eyes closed. The old crab, taken by surprise, waited a moment and then reaching out one of his feet pushed the crab. The old crab, talking to himself in a muffled voice, muttered, "It's only the shell. It's empty. Well, he wasn't much anyway."

The baby crab closed his eyes and remained quiet.

After the old crab had left, the baby crab heard the sound of the crabs mingled with the sound of the falling rain, as they marched to the sea. In his mind's eye he would see the crabs floating on the water and then crawling on the river bottom. The old crab was in the midst of the others and beside him he saw himself crawling down to the river. He was crawling sideways.

The Touch of Life

by Pak Yong-jun
translated by Genell Y. Poitras

"My son, my son why did you have to die. . . ."

Chong-hae heaved a sigh as he sat beside the body of his son. A whole day had passed since his son's death. Since he had told no one he had only himself to blame that not a single person came to call. He would have to make all of the funeral arrangements by himself. Although the registering of the death and the final plans were up to him, and in spite of the fact that he had deliberately avoided making friends, Chong-hae still seemed pathetic.

"My son, my son. . ."

Again, he blamed his son. This was his son's last year of high school and next year he planned to send him to college in one way or another. How could his son have died even before he had taken his college entrance exams? The only child! What was worse was that he was the only heir in the whole family. Now that his son was old enough to help his father, who was almost fifty, what did he do but die. There was no one to run the errands. On the contrary, his son's burial arrangements were left to him.

If the truth be known, the main reason that Chong-hae was looking forward to his son's growing up was with the expectation that he would take over more of the household chores. His wife had left him fifteen years ago and he never remarried but continued to live alone. His widowed sister came to take care of them but she was less then resourceful and couldn't even prepare the food without being told what to do. Chong-hae also took responsibility for the fuel and clothing. Why did his son have to die just when he was able to help around the house? Then, too, he was left with all of the funeral arrangements as well. Since this was his only son who would help him during the rest of his life?

Chong-hae's sister kept vigil with him. Now and then she stared at him. Even though the death of a young man is hard. She thought to herself that it wasn't right if no one came to pay respects.

A whole day passed. Not even one person came to call. Her eyes clearly showed how she felt about her brother's behavior. He should have told his neighbors and fellow teachers. The family had no immediate relatives in Seoul who needed to be told, but surely he had an obligation to tell his fellow teachers with whom he had been working for some twenty years.

Chong-hae didn't tell the neighbors because he disliked the idea of anyone coming to the house to offer condolences. He wouldn't allow his sister to wail since this would indicate to the neighbors that there had been a death in the family. His sister was unable to understand his reasoning. She wondered if there could be anyone in the world who thought like that. Although she was concerned about informing others, at this point, she was more worried as to how she would feed anyone who might come.

"Don't you think we should fix some food?" she asked as

she carefully watched her brother's face.

"Why are you worried about food when there aren't any callers?" he retorted, as if to say she was just making problems for no reason at all.

"Well, even if no one comes don't we still have to go through with the service? Don't we have to feed the people who help out?"

"Why should we be obliged to others when for a few pennies we can hire men to help?"

"In a house where people are still living is it right if no one comes? Suppose you have just one day left to live, you still shouldn't do things that others will criticize you for. If we don't do anything else, at least please let's fix some food."

"All right. I'll go out and buy something," he said as he jumped up and left. He was reluctant to discuss the matter any more as he knew all too well that the two of them could never agree.

It didn't seem right to Chong-hae to talk about food just after the death of a loved one. The most important thing was to comfort the bereaved. He disliked sham of any kind. The success of a funeral celebration was not to be judged by the amount of food. Those who were truly sympathetic would come whether or not food was served. They could shed tears together without drinking and eating.

Chong-hae had no close friend with whom he could share his grief. He didn't want anyone to come who would just sit around waiting for the food to be served. He disliked senseless arguments with his sister. Although he said he was going to the market, he went directly to his school.

He went to the personnel office first to report his absence. "I've been away from school because my son was suddenly taken ill. I'm afraid that I'll have to be gone tomorrow, too."

On his way to the business office he tried to avoid meeting any of his fellow teachers. At the office he said to the accountant, "My son is critically ill and it looks as if he'll have to go to the hospital. Would you be so kind as to give me an advance on my salary?"

The accountant looked surprised and asked, "What seems to be the matter?"

"It looks as though he caught pneumonia on top of some intestinal flu." Chong-hae replied, as he in fact described the cause of his son's death.

"That's too bad. Better have it taken care of right away. No need to worry though because now there's good medicine for pneumonia. Wait a moment please."

The accountant seemed flustered as he hurriedly wrote something on a slip of paper and went out of the office to get the request approved. After a long time he returned with the authorization. He said nothing as he put the slip down. Then taking out a sheaf of bills, he started to count. He counted out the right amount and gave it to Chong-hae saying, "If you need more come and ask anytime."

Like a thief, who has stolen money and tries to wrap it hurriedly, he stuffed the money in one pocket and then in another. He was afraid that anyone seeing him with so much money might think that he had come by it dishonestly. Although he had been teaching for nearly twenty years this was the first time he asked for so much salary in advance.

Chong-hae felt relieved that it wasn't necessary to mention his son's death. If he let the news of his son's death out he would have to tell everyone, friends and mere acquaintances. He would have to look sad and talk in a solemn tone of voice. Then, too, they would comment about how terrible it was and also that he didn't have anymore children. Even the most insincere one would have to pretend to be sympathetic. There was nothing that he detested more than this kind of hypocrisy. Of course, when there is a death in the family, people are supposed to look sad even though they may not feel that way.

At that moment Chong-hae felt a sense of elation that as a human being he, like some God, could detach himself from this earthly scene.

There would be no need to tell anyone in the future either.

The death of his son meant nothing to anyone else. A sympathetic response when he might announce his son's death would be so momentary; like a stone by the side of the road that is noted in passing and then immediately forgotten. What use would it be to insist on that kind of a response?

Chong-hae went from the school to the hospital where he had purchased medicine for his son, in order to get the medical certification of the death. This he presented at the city hall where he received a death certificate and a cremation permit. Next he stopped at the Hongje Crematorium to make arrangements for his son's cremation. On his way home he stopped at the undertaker to order the funeral car to pick up his son's body.

All day he had been busily making the burial arrangements so that by the time he arrived home night had come. He entered the house. His sister was sitting beside the corpse, crying as if her heart would break, as she fondled the hands and feet of her nephew. Chong-hae wasn't sure but that her tears were more for herself than his son. She was sixty already and didn't have many years left. The way in which she handled the body as she wailed didn't appear to be out of regret for her nephew's death, but rather, that she felt she had been put under a curse. The sight of his sister crying made him swell with resentment. Of course, it was right for her to be sad and to cry, but why did she have to put her hands all over his son's body? His son's body belonged to him.

Once in the past he had experienced this same feeling when one of the teachers had taken his cigarette lighter. He couldn't find his lighter. It wasn't expensive but he felt lost without it. Where could it have gone? He had used the lighter during the morning. While he was searching for it one of the teachers saw him and suggested that perhaps someone had taken it. Chong-hae flushed with anger at the thought of anyone taking something that didn't belong to him without first asking permission. He, himself, had never so much as coveted the property of another.

After school was over he hurriedly straightened his desk and went directly to the home of the teacher who had suggested that someone may have taken the lighter. The teacher had taken it only to tease Chong-hae. When he saw that Chong-hae had made a special trip to get it back he sneered, and said, "You're making a mountain out of a mole hill. Is your lighter worth that much?"

"It doesn't matter about the value of it. The important thing is that it's mine," answered Chong-hae as he took the lighter and returned home.

By this time tomorrow his son's body would be gone. However, up until that time the body was his. His own flesh and blood. He had raised him. All day he busied himself making the burial arrangements and not even one tiny ant had helped him. He went alone to the city hall, to the crematorium and to the undertaker.

"Give me my supper," he angrily ordered his sister.

She looked embarrassed, as if she had been caught in the act of stealing. She wiped her eyes and pretended as if she hadn't been crying. She walked hurriedly toward the kitchen.

Four days had gone by since his son's body had been cremated. After many hours of deliberation, Chong-hae decided to tell his principal. He had been resisting telling anyone because he didn't want to feel forced to do so. However, he felt apprehensive about telling the principal at this late date.

He wondered whether anyone gives any more thought to the death of another's child than to the kicking of a stone by the side of the road. Now that his son was dead and gone, why did he still wonder whether or not to tell the other teachers? He knew that if he had told them at the time they would have reacted emotionally and this he disliked. Although it was too late for any sincere expression of sympathy he felt that he must tell them now or risk greater reproof later. Besides, the teachers at his school had established a mutual aid fund to help member families in time of need. Each one contributed to the fund monthly and then had the privilege of drawing from the fund when needed. If Chong-hae didn't inform the school of his son's death, he couldn't use the fund. Was there any reason for him alone not to benefit?

He went into the principal's office and announced, "Sooner or later you're going to find out that my son has died. We've already had the funeral. I didn't want to anything at the time because I knew that everyone was busy and I didn't want to bother anyone."

"What do you mean? How could you keep something like that to yourself?" asked the principal.

The principal reacted just as Chong-hae had anticipated. His facial expression showed that he didn't think it right for Chong-hae not to have told him at the time.

"Well, what use would it have been if I had told you at the time? Your mind rests easier when you don't know."

"Mr. Kang, I don't understand you at all. It's natural to share one's sorrow with others. You're too much of a loner. You'd better change."

"Yes," replied Chong-hae, hanging his head. But, of course, the principal was right. Deep down inside he wondered how a man of fifty could change. He shrugged his shoulders.

Up until now he had lived a lonely life. Though he stood to lose a great deal by not announcing his son's death it seemed too late to try to change his personality.

Chong-hae tried to look penitent as the principal continued to scold him. He knew that in order to put an end to the scolding he must do so even though he didn't feel that he had done anything wrong.

"The other teachers will be sad to hear the news so you'd better go and tell them quickly," instructed the principal. He seemed sincere and horrified, at the same time, by Chong-hae's behavior.

Chong-hae sensed that he had been dismissed and replied that he would tell the other teachers. He hurriedly left the office and went directly to the faculty lounge. However, he kept silent and said nothing about his son.

At the time of a funeral those who are only superficially sympathetic are at a loss as to the proper way in which to express their emotions. They will feel a certain sense of relief when the funeral is over. Yet at the same time, these same people would make a great fuss when learning about the event afterward and say that things are just not done in that way. How could he open up in front of people like this?

The more he thought about it the more inclined he was to say nothing, even though he had promised the principal that he would. He left school before classes were finished.

He hated the thought of going home. Suddenly his room had become like a prison cell and overflowed with loneliness. He was afraid. Instead of going home he headed for the department store. He recalled that his son had wanted a watch. He had stubbornly refused to buy him a watch until he was ready to enter college. He hated himself and regretted his actions.

He entered the store and went to the watch counter where he saw many inexpensive watches. He muttered to himself, "Does anyone know when he'll die?"

If he had known that his son was going to die there wouldn't have been any reason not to have bought him one of the inexpensive watches. He looked at the watches and went so far as to ask the price of the ones he liked.

The clerk picked up the one that Chong-hae liked and said, "This is a good one and has a three year guaranty."

As the clerk started to wind the watch Chong-hae said, "But, there is no one to give it to." He muttered something about coming back again and walked out of the store.

He started for home. However, when he remembered that the son who had begged for the watch was no longer there he couldn't force himself to go home. Instead he started to wander aimlessly in the street. He didn't know where he was going.

In this despondent state he crossed an alley and found himself unexpectedly in front of a tavern. He felt a sudden urge to have a drink. Without any hesitation he entered and ordered a glass of beer. The bar maid who also made the lentil pancakes brought him some on a plate with a glass of beer. As he tilted the glass to have a drink he wondered why he hadn't thought about having a drink before this. He drank half of the glass. As he put the glass down on the table he heaved a sigh without being aware of it.

One of the bartenders put a plate of pancakes down in front of another customer and then stopped at his table and asked, "Say, aren't you Chong-hae?"

The man's hair was long and unkempt. His clothes were shabby. Chong-hae couldn't decide whether he was the owner of the place or just an errand boy. He couldn't bring himself to ask. As he stared at the man he suddenly realized who he was.

"Don't you know who I am? I'm Myŏng-u," he said as he shrugged his shoulders in amazement that Chong-hae didn't recognize him.

"Oh, but of course, Myŏng-u," Chong-hae replied. At the same time he recalled that Kim Myŏng-u had been a middle school classmate. His enemy from out of the past. He froze in his chair. It was like meeting an enemy on a one-way bridge, there was no way to avoid him.

"How long has it been since we last met? About twenty years or so. So that is why you didn't recognize me." Myŏng-u seemed genuinely glad to see him and put out his hand. What could Chong-hae do but apologize and shake hands. "How are things going with you? I heard that you are a school teacher."

"Yes, I manage to make a living somehow."

"I also heard that you had lost your wife and that you hadn't gotten married again. Is that so?"

"Yes, that's right."

They had been classmates some twenty years ago and yet Chong-hae barely replied to Myŏng-u's questions. A problem between them in the past had left them with bad feelings.

"Look at me. Here I am running a tavern. During all of these years I've tried various jobs but failed in every single one.

Last year I started this place." Myŏng-u talked on and on. He needed no encouragement. Chong-hae sensed that if he just left him alone he would readily reveal his whole past.

Chong-hae disliked garrulous people. He emptied the glass in his hand, shoved it at Myŏng-u and said, "Let's have a drink together in celebration."

"Well, if you're buying, of course I'll have one. Who would've dreamed that you would be buying me a drink," chattered Myŏng-u. In a loud voice he called to the woman who was cooking the pancakes to bring some beer.

As she approached the table he asked her. "Hey old lady, don't you know Chong-hae? We were classmates and we haven't seen each other in twenty years. He was the one who brought that lawsuit against me. Remember? Well, that's all past so we don't need to mention it. So just forget it. Hurry up and say hello to him."

Chong-hae rose from his chair. There was no way that he could avoid saying hello to her. He stifled an impulse to slap Myŏng-u in the face and sat down.

"I'll bring some rice wine," she said as she left the table.

"Okay, let's pass around the glass." Myong-u was the kind of a person who said whatever came into his head. He gave no thought as to the effect of his words on his listeners. Chong-hae disliked people who didn't think before they spoke.

He finished another glass of wine and said as he got up from his chair, "I have some urgent business to attend to so I must be going."

During all of that time Myŏng-u hadn't forgotten that Chong-hae had brought that lawsuit against him. Although Chong-hae felt uncomfortable in Myŏng-u's presence it seemed obvious that Myŏng-u didn't hold a grudge against him. Chong-hae brought a suit against his friend for the sake of a fifty *hwan* loan.

He began to have the uneasy feeling that the whole human race was judging him. Even so, Chong-hae couldn't bring himself to forgive his friend for not having returned the money he had borrowed. He had even gone so far as to call in the law in order to get back the loan. Chong-hae had won but the cost was high. He had decided, once and for all, that it was unnecessary to suffer that much ever again when he had acted in all sincerity. He would trust no one, nor would he expect trust in return.

From then on he lived a solitary and lonely existence according to this creed. At the time he had even thought of putting a seizure on Myŏng-u's property before the money was returned. That fifty *hwan* had created a deep chasm in his heart which nothing, not even sincere regret, could erase.

Except for a chance meeting Chong-hae hoped that he would never meet Myŏng-u again. The best thing would be to end this chance meeting as quickly as possible.

He got up from his chair. He knew that he should pay for his drink but he couldn't bring himself to ask how much he owed. Would Myŏng-u even take the money? He had no desire to have a drink on the house. He calculated the cost in his head. Three glasses of beer would come to one hundred and fifty *hwan*, and adding one plate of lentil pancakes at fifty *hwan* would make two hundred in all. Although the amount seemed ample he was unsure of the cost of the pancakes. He didn't want to be accused of being stingy. Even the most expensive pancakes wouldn't be more than one hundred *hwan* so two hundred and fifty *hwan* should be more than enough. He dug in his pockets but all he could find was three hundred *hwan*. He thought that was more than enough as he tossed the bills down in front of Myŏng-u. He suggested that they meet again, said goodbye and left. As he came outside he felt sure that Myŏng-u would chase after him with the change and scold him for not waiting. A person like Myŏng-u was more generous than a person like himself who could only feel free once a debt was settled.

As he expected, Myŏng-u called to him. He was sure that he had figured correctly. He wanted to sever all ties with the past so he didn't turn around. He pretended not to hear as he kept on walking. How could anyone who had brought a lawsuit against another ever take a free drink from that person?

Before he could get very far Myŏng-u caught up with him, slapped him on the shoulder and handed him the money saying, "You forgot your change, fifty *hwan*."

The account was settled. All was fair and square. Chong-hae's heart felt light. "If beer is so cheap I'll have to come again," he said as he took the money, put it in his pocket, and walked away.

He hadn't gone far before he retraced his steps. He felt good that the account was settled forever. Now he could begin again with the change. He had an overwhelming desire to spend the money immediately. Once again he entered the tavern. He ordered a glass of beer. Myŏng-u smiled broadly as he brought him a glass of beer and also a dish of *kimchi*. Chong-hae quickly gulped down the beer and as he left said that the beer was good. Once again he started out for home.

Whether or not the drinks had anything to do with it, he was overcome with emotion when he returned home. "My one and only child is gone," he sobbed as he tried to stifle the tears. Why should he? He could cry as much as he wished. However, he couldn't erase from his mind his recent encounter with Myŏng-u and he hardly felt right about crying.

He and his estranged wife had been married less than a year when he loaned his wife's dowry to Myŏng-u so that he could get married. He did feel uneasy about lending his wife's money but since it was for a wedding he had persuaded her. They lent the money believing that it would be repayed within two months as Myŏng-u had promised at the time. Then, too, Chong-hae firmly believed that money used for a wedding was special and should be settled before any other debts.

Six months passed. And, still Myŏng-u hadn't repayed the loan. Several months later he disappeared without a word. Upon inquiry Chong-hae discovered that he wasn't the only one who had lent him money. He felt apologetic to his young wife; he hadn't even been able to afford a ring when they had been married. It made him so miserable to think about the money his wife had carefully guarded, and which he had loaned and lost, that he brought a lawsuit against his friend. His wife questioned it and tried to stop him. But, he insisted that he had been provoked into doing it. He not only filed a lawsuit but he even intended to place a seizure on Myŏng-u's property. He wanted to shower the worst possible insult on this scoundrel who had betrayed his trust. However, the money was paid back before he could resort to this action.

His wife chided him, "Would you have starved without that money? You're the only one that is out if you lose a friend for the sake of fifty *hwan.*"

He regretted more than ever that he had taken the money. His wife's words of some twenty years ago were as clear to him now as if she had said them only yesterday. He seemed to hear a voice from the distance saying, "The time will come when you will seek out the very person from whom you were alienated in the past."

This chance meeting with Myŏng-u recalled to his memory thoughts of his wife. Wherever she was she would be happy to know that he had met Myŏng-u once again. As he thought about her he remembered what she had done to him. He shrugged his shoulders. She had a respectable husband and a child. Yet, she became attached to another so that Chong-hae was forced to drive her away. How many bitter tears had he shed because of her? The tears flowed without ceasing as he cared for his small baby boy.

He was only thirty when they parted and he had never remarried. Did he still have a lingering attachment for her? How small of him to be nursing these resentments. He was no better than a worm. Until today he had cursed his desire for his wife, and now for the first time in twenty years he felt as if he had made her happy. For a split second he felt an unpleasant feeling inside. As he thought about his wife he again hated Myŏng-u. But, he told himself that he must not let this feeling interfere with the chance to think once again about his relationship with Myŏng-u.

He was nauseated by the sight of Myŏng-u running after him to return his change. He felt an urge to spit in his face. The problem over the fifty *hwan* seemed to be chasing after him for retaliation. Did he get his revenge? No, all of those lonely years had been a waste and he was the loser.

It was too late to wonder why he had lived such a lonely life. He yearned all the more for his dead son. He told himself that were his son still alive they wouldn't live as poorly as they had. Tears began to fall. He didn't wipe them away. His son's death had made a farce of his own life.

Just when he finally gained control of himself several members of the school faculty came to call. They brought a bottle of wine and said there was no need to be sad now that his son was dead and gone. They suggested that they drink together in order to help him to forget his sorrow. Chong-hae thanked them. Whether or not they drank together he was touched by their desire to help him forget his grief. He couldn't remember when he had last felt thankful to anyone. He was about to ask his sister to bring out the glasses when, like the principal, they began to reprove him for not having told them in the beginning about his son's death. The thankful feeling vanished. As they handed him an envelope from the mutual aid fund he suddenly realized why they had come. He accepted the money only because he had a right to it. Any desire that he had of sitting down and drinking together entirely disappeared. It was apparent from the expression on the face of one of the teachers as he glances at the wine bottle that he wondered where the wine glasses were.

Chong-hae noticed the look and excused himself saying, "I haven't slept for several nights. I'm really bushed. Forgive me if I don't invite you in."

They said goodbye and left. Although it must have seemed thoughtless he hardly felt he must talk at length with people who came only out of a sense of duty.

No sooner had he sent them away than he sensed an

emptiness welling up inside which was different from the sorrow he had felt at his son's death. His cold, calculated philosophy of life allowed for no weak spot where hurt might be inflicted. For the first time in twenty years this outer surface had cracked and this feeling of emptiness was the inner response to his loneliness. He was unable to interpret the reason for his heartache. All he knew was that he was suddenly engulfed in a vast sea of emptiness.

He did not go to school the next day. He was more conscientious than any other teacher and never missed. For the first time in twenty years he did not live according to his creed. He began to see that living so as not to hurt anyone or not to be hurt in return was contrary to human nature. He spent the whole day in bed. Was it because there was nothing left of him but a shell enclosing an empty heart? Then, too, he had the strange feeling that his body was floating in space.

His sister was obviously concerned to see him staying in bed all day and questioned him in a worried tone of voice, "If you don't feel well shouldn't you go to the hospital?" Only a few short days ago she had grieved for her nephew. Now it seemed perfectly natural to her to be panic-stricken over her brother's condition.

"No need to worry, I won't up and die on you," he replied in a quarrelsome manner.

"If you die what is left? Shouldn't you worry about your own body?" she said without understanding his behavior.

"Who worries about his own body after he is dead?" he argued.

She did not respond but began to cry.

Chong-hae was unwilling to acknowledge her concern and reproved her, "Now who's died that you're carrying on like this?"

"No matter what I say or do you hate me. So you're just waiting for me to die and because I am still around you talk this way." Her crying became more sorrowful.

"Sister, who told you to up and die? I suppose you take me

for some kind of undertaker or something."

His sister had done nothing wrong during her entire life. He knowingly tormented her without any reason and ended up by making her feel completely rejected.

"Stop talking like that. Life is sad enough. What sin have I committed other than begging for food or just eating off of you?"

These words were enough to silence him. Finally he understood. Sin, to her, was eating off of someone else. There was a great similarity in the depressing plight of each of their lives.

They had been silent for sometime when they heard a knock at the gate. His sister got up to go out and open the gate.

In a softer tone of voice Chong-hae said to her, "I don't want to see anyone so say that I'm not feeling well and that I'm lying down." This was the first time he had asked for help. The expression on his sister's face showed that she understood and she went out to open the gate.

His sister talked to someone at the gate for what seemed like an eternity. Then she came into the room and held out an envelope to him and said, "A teacher from Ch'un-kyu's school brought this for you."

"What is it?"

"Well, he said that it was one of Ch'un-kyu's papers."

Chong-hae bolted out of bed, took the envelope and went out to ask his son's teacher to come in. As soon as the teacher greeted him Chong-hae could tell by his face that he felt truly sorry about Ch'un-kyu's death.

His son had written an essay on his last day of school and since the teacher had no need to keep it he brought it to Chong-hae. Chong-hae thanked him and invited him to come in. The other teachers tried to show their sympathy with money while this teacher came because he had liked Ch'un-kyu and also seemed to understand the father's feelings.

He turned to his sister and asked her to bring the wine glasses. However, the teacher excused himself by saying that he had work to do. He turned around and left.

After the teacher had left he felt compelled to take his son's essay out of the envelope. He began to read.

I don't have a mother. I mean, I don't know whether she is dead or alive. My father says that she is dead, but my aunt's look tells me that she must be alive somewhere. If my father tells me that my mother who is actually alive, is dead, than that must mean that she is a bad person and I shouldn't know her. However, I long for my mother. Even though she may not be a good person, I would like to see her, just once. I want to meet my mother more than I want to meet any famous person. Perhaps my desire is similar to the tiny baby's yearning for its mother's breast. But, that is not what I want. I don't need her breast, nor do I need anything. The only thing that I want is to merely smell her. I don't care whether the smell is pleasant or not. Even if the smell is bad I want to smell my mother at least once before I die.

He stopped reading, folded the composition and put it on the floor. He couldn't continue because he was afraid of what might follow. He got into his bed as he muttered to himself, "No matter how you look at it, the father's love is not enough."

The longer he thought about his son's longing for his mother, the more he came to the realization that food alone was not enough to satisfy the empty feeling within the soul. Although he might have tried, for his son's sake, to have preserved the image of his wife, he couldn't help but resent her for having run off with another man. So illness alone was not the cause of his son's death. He died yearning for his mother's nearness, her smell, her touch.

As the day wore on the emptiness in his breast gave way to a satisfied feeling. He wondered if this feeling was the result of his new awareness that the ambiguity of his son's death, which had at first made him feel lonely and depressed, had been replaced by the new knowledge that the death had other causes.

Suddenly he was seized with a strong desire for a drink. He got up from his bed and changed his clothes. Actually, he didn't want a drink. Just as his son had yearned for his mother's nearness, he, too, felt the need for the touch of another human being.

Where did he go but to Myŏng-u's tavern. All of a sudden, the thought that Myŏng-u might have returned the change only to get even crossed his mind. However, that seemed impossible as Myŏng-u wasn't the kind of a person who held a grudge. Because he had deceived Chong-hae when he was destitute didn't mean that he was a bad person. Furthermore, a person like that wouldn't be running a tavern. Chong-hae came to the conclusion that Myŏng-u had returned the change because he was trying to live an honest life. His sudden desire to seek out Myŏng-u was an indication of his unconscious need for human companionship.

"Good. Glad you came. But, why didn't you bring your friends? Why did you come alone?" Myŏng-u seemed glad enough to see him but it was apparent that he knew Chong-hae wouldn't bring him much business. Chong-hae liked frankness. He was right. Myŏng-u was that kind of a person.

"Well, sure. Next time I'll try to drag all of my school buddies along," replied Chong-hae.

"Why go elsewhere? Drinks are all the same price. Help out your friends."

"Of course, you're right," answered Chong-hae as he tried to make himself agreeable. After one drink he asked Myŏng-u about his children. He even volunteered the information that he himself had lost his only son several days earlier.

"No! Not your only son!" Myŏng-u exclaimed with a

shocked expression on his face. He meant it. The feeling came from his heart.

"He was only eighteen. Up until the time of his death we had been making plans for his college entrance next year."

"When did he die?"

"About four or five days ago."

"Four or five days ago! Then why didn't you say something when you came in yesterday?"

He was just like the principal and the faculty who blamed him for not having told them sooner. However Myŏng-u's accusation seemed different. He wasn't blaming Chong-hae or trying to take advantage of the situation.

"Well, if you had known what would you have done?"

"Who in the world thinks like that? During our whole lifetime and up until the time we die do we share with others only when we expect something in return? Don't you feel a need to tell someone even though they can't help you?"

"Yes. I'm sorry. You're absolutely right." The idea of sharing without the expectation of receiving any help appealed to Chong-hae. He didn't know the reason why his shoulders drooped. Myŏng-u had deeper insight than he in every situation.

Chong-hae drank several glasses of beer and as he got up from his chair he announced, "Next time I'll be sure to bring my friends."

"Yes, help me out. Friends need to help each other out you know. Isn't that what friendship means?"

Chong-hae feigned drunkedness as he slapped Myŏng-u on the shoulders. He started to talk in the schoolboy slang they had used years ago.

"Yes, yes, this fool finally sees the light."

"You son-of-a-bitch. What do you know anyway? You don't even know bullshit," retorted Myŏng-u.

"Why you son-of-a-gun. Better not talk like that. Who talks fresh like that to an adult anyhow. Ha, ha, ha."

"Look at you. Talking to your elder brother like that.

You're not even dry behind the ears. It's going to be a long time before you grow up. Ha, ha, ha."

Their voices grew louder and louder as they laughed. Could this be the very first time in twenty years that Chong-hae had laughed so heartily.

"You son-of-a-bitch, what's the damage?"

"Same as yesterday. Give me three hundred *hwan* and I'll give you fifty in change."

"No, three hundred is fine. Give the change to your wife for a tip. Understand? I know it seems odd to give a tip to one's sister-in-law, but, after all, she is a waitress, so what."

"Watch your tongue, you son-of-a-bitch, when you talk about your elder brother's wife."

Once again they laughed long and hard.

Chong-hae paid for the drinks, and left without expecting any change. Myŏng-u followed after him.

"Don't take it so hard. After all, the living must live," he said. "Next time it's my treat. Come again and have red hot pepper stew. My wife's not a bad cook. It's good."

Chong-hae already felt good inside at Myŏng-u's offer to treat him. He felt an even closer bond when Myŏng-u praised his own wife's cooking.

"Say, where is the fool who boasts about his wife's cooking?" Chong-hae smiled from ear to ear as he joked and laughed.

"Not at all. The one who has no wife is the fool. Right? So who's the fool after all?" retorted Myŏng-u as he gave Chong-hae a shove. There was no doubt in his mind who was the fool.

Startled, Chong-hae took a step backwards. "Why you son-of-a-gun. You smell. Don't touch me," he said as he took his hand and brushed off the place where Myŏng-u had touched him. He felt a strong desire, however, to secretly put his nose to the place where Myŏng-u's hand had touched his shoulder.

He turned around as he started to walk away and said,

"Just wait and see what happens if you don't make good on that promise."

Chong-hae smiled to himself as he walked away.